TRIBAL LAW

IS THE LAW STRONGER THAN LOVE

By Dave H Jordan

DEDICATIONS

THIS BOOK IS INSPIRED BY AND DEDICATED FIRST TO GOD AND MY LORD AND SAVIOR JESUS CHRIST FOR LOVING ME AND BLESSING ME WITH THE GIFT AND WITH THE LOVE OF MY LIFE; AND SECOND, TO MY BEAUTIFUL, LOVING AND ENDURING WIFE, TRISH, WHOSE LOVE CONTINUALLY INSPIRES ME TO BE MORE THAN I AM AND TEACHES ME MORE ABOUT LOVE EVERY DAY OF MY LIFE

Contents

Part 4: Sacrifice, Commitments and Death

Part 5: Blood, Sweat and Tears

PROLOGUE

It has been exactly one year since Marcus and Zephora first met, and today is the day they have both long awaited. This is the day they are to be wed. Both Marcus and Zephora had to overcome many obstacles to be here, and surely it was more than fate that brought them together. Today, all their hopes and dreams are culminating with their union.

There on the front row of the right side of the church sits Zephora's only known living relative, her mother, Saphera, whose eyes are filled with tears of joy because finally, peace has come to their little family of two, and she has never seen her daughter happier. Saphera wishes Zephora's father could have lived to see this moment, but it just wasn't in the cards. One day she will have to tell Zephora all about her family heritage.

As Marcus stands next to his best man, Angelo, who also doubles as his oldest and most trusted friend, he looks down at his sister, Charlie, his father, Jackson; and then stares at his grandmother, Ruth, whose infinite wisdom has gotten him through more than his share of challenges, and inspired countless smiles. Now, it's his turn to enthuse a smile; not just a simple smile, but the kind of smile that says "I'm okay, I've

1

found her, the perfect woman, and I couldn't be happier." It also says I'm nervous as heck, too; however, only Ruth recognizes his nervousness.

It's New Year's Eve, and Marcus and Zephora are about to send the old year out on a high note, and welcome the new one in with a bang. It's 7:58 p.m. and the bride, the maid of honor, the ring bearer, and the flower girl are standing at the outer door to the sanctuary.

PART 1

HOLY MATRIMONY

CHAPTER I

Standing nervously at the altar, with Angelo by his side, Marcus turns and looks left to see the doors of the sanctuary begin to open and Marcus' mind starts to race and his pulse begins to hasten.

"This is it," he thinks to himself, "the moment of truth. Oh my God! I hope I'm ready for this. There's no turning back now; too late for me to back out." Then he brings his thoughts under control. "Back out!? No way! I have the most incredible woman ever, waiting behind those doors to become my wife. She's smart, beautiful, and fine, and has a smile that could singlehandedly start global warming; yeah, I'm ready. I think." He loses it once more and becomes nervous all over again; this time almost to the point of nausea. "Breathe, breathe, breathe," he tells himself. "I can handle this. This is nothing. I have waited for this moment for this perfect woman my entire life; the one person who loves me for me, and isn't trying to change me into a robot husband - yes honey, sure honey, right away honey. Shoot, she even laughs at my jokes. She isn't stuck up or insecure. She's perfect for me. I can be attached and free all at the same time. Hallelujah, praise God, let's do this, I'm ready!!"

Marcus has had his share of crazy women. To find one who is seemingly so complete, well, to say the least, that is a dream come true for him. As he stands waiting for his bride to come through those doors, his mind wanders back through the long list of women he once loved. And though he loved them all, on some level, none of them were right for him. Each of them, in their own way, tried to change him to fit their description of what they thought a man should be. He wasted years at a time trying to make them happy, and at times to his own detriment. Marcus was the type of guy who loved hard and fast, which is always a recipe for pain especially when you aren't loving the one person that was meant for you. Maybe all those lost loves prepared him for this special one.

With Zephora, things are different. He knows without a shadow of a doubt that this woman was made for him and no one else. Before Zephora, he chose the women that were in his life, and the result was always the same, tragic endings. However, two years ago he re-membered himself to the Body of Christ, and in doing so, he made a commitment to work hard at becoming a righteous man each and every day of his life. And, it was at that time that God chose to let Marcus know that when he was ready and the woman He made for him was ready, He would tug on Marcus' left ear and point her out to Marcus. And that is exactly what God did, and exactly why

Marcus knows Zephora was made for him. And now standing here at the alter awaiting his bride, Marcus can't help but think back and reminisce about how all this came to be.

"After all the women I chose for myself and took advantage of, that were so very wrong for me, it's hard to believe God has forgiven me and still loves me enough to make this woman specifically and especially for me. I'll never forget how He let me know she was the one." Zephora invited Marcus and his friend JT to a party. They were all friends so there was nothing unusual about it. A group of them had been hanging out for a month or so and had all become pretty good friends, especially Marcus and Zephora. They could talk all night about everything, anything or nothing. On one such occasion, Marcus told JT that Zephora was the most complete woman he had ever met. Man, she's gonna make somebody an excellent wife one day," Marcus remarked to JT. However, he had never considered her for himself; he didn't think he was worthy of such a graceful and majestic woman. However, God chose that night to let him know he was indeed worthy. When God tugged on Marcus' ear, he turned to see who was touching him, but no one was close enough to him to touch him. When he turned his head back around, God said to him in a quiet still voice "*THAT IS THE WOMAN I MADE FOR YOU,*" in his mind's eye he could see a finger attached to a hand and an arm up to the elbow pointing and directing his attention towards Zephora. "Who, Zephora?," Marcus replied. "*YES,*" God's voice resounded. "Are you sure?" Marcus retorted. "*YES,*" God reiterated. "WOW!" Marcus exclaimed. "I knew she would make someone an incredible wife, I just never thought in a million years it would ever be me." Now, the time is here for Zephora to get ready to walk down the aisle to the man she was created for and he is excited and scared all in one. "I guess dreams do come true. Thank You, God, I am finally gonna get to the good part," Marcus thought to himself.

After Marcus' tortured past, it felt good to finally be getting to the good part. Although both of Marcus' parents are alive, they have been divorced since he was five, his big sister Charlie was nine, and his baby sister Nicolette, God rest her soul, was still in the womb. You see, Marcus' father, Jackson Howard, was an abusive husband. When Marcus' mother, Esther, couldn't take it anymore, she made a daring escape and took the kids and relocated. Marcus was about three and a half years old at that time. A year later, Jackson followed and rejoined the family with promises of making everything right again. Six months later, Jackson decided he didn't want to be tied down to a wife and three kids, and Jackson packed his bags and quietly tipped out during the night. In his haste to abandon his family, he didn't notice Marcus watching him from his bedroom window.

After that night, Esther became a mean and bitter woman, and since Jackson was no longer around, Esther's anger was directed toward her kids. She never missed a moment to tell them how good for nothing their father was. She became an abusive parent, at times literally beating the blood out of Charlie and Marcus. After a few years of the constant abuse, Charlie couldn't take it anymore. She resourcefully found her father, whom she loved very much, and begged him to let her come and live with him. The beatings from her mother were getting worse and she feared for her life. Six months later Charlie left to be with her father, seemingly without any regard for Marcus' and Nicolette's wellbeing. Marcus found out some time later that in Charlie's mind, she thought it would make things better for them if she left. Boy was she wrong.

With Charlie gone, Esther now focused her complete anger towards Marcus, who just happened to be the spitting image of his father. There was nowhere for Marcus to go. He despised his father for abandoning them, and was afraid of his mother and her wrath. Besides, what would happen to Nicolette? Unbeknown to him, he wouldn't have to worry about her that much longer, because shortly after Nicolette's fourth birthday, she went to sleep one night, and never woke up again. Marcus was devastated. He loved his little sister so much; she was the only friend he had. No official cause of death was ever known, it was as if her little heart literally broke into a million pieces and stopped working. Even though Esther was visibly upset, she didn't seem to be nearly as devastated as Marcus thought she should be and definitely not shattered as much as he was. The funeral came and went and there was no word from Charlie or his father. He was truly alone now and his anger was beginning to turn to hate. What Marcus didn't know was that Esther had concealed the news of Nicolette's death from his sister and father. Esther also withheld from Marcus all the letters that Charlie had written to him since she left. His only break from loneliness and the abuse he suffered would come when he and his mother would visit his grandmother, Ruth. Ruth is Esther's mother and in Marcus' eyes the wisest, most intelligent woman he had ever known.

For Marcus' sixteenth birthday, he got a surprise visit from Charlie whom he hadn't seen or heard from in eight years. Charlie, then twenty and in the military, nearly had a nervous breakdown when she found out about Nicolette. She blamed herself and it took Marcus days to console her. When she asked why he never wrote her back, she was shocked to find out he never received any of her letters. Charlie had no words for Esther. She begged Marcus to leave and go away with her. Marcus refused and decided to stay and finish high school. He wasn't afraid of Esther anymore and Esther knew it and mostly stayed out of his way. It would be four more years before he heard from Charlie again, and this time, Charlie had a plan to bring her father and brother together; however, Marcus wanted no part of this. He was an adult now, a college student, and he didn't have the need for a father and definitely not his father. But because he loved Charlie, he agreed to meet Jackson. Jackson gave his best worst remorseful apology, but it was too little, too late. However, Marcus' strong sense of family forced him to make amends. He has been fostering a relationship with Jackson ever since. As for Esther, he checks on her from time to time, but they may never be close, especially with all of her deceptive ways exposed. He did however; invite her to this joyous occasion.

It's almost show time. Marcus turns toward his best man and smiles. "Good old Angelo. Thank you God for him, too," Marcus thinks to himself. Upon entering high school, Marcus met Angelo. They instantly became best friends, and have been that way ever since. He couldn't ask for a better man to be his best friend. He has never judged Marcus. "Even when I screw up royally, he never judges me, but is always there no matter what happens. I hope I am as good a friend to him as he is to me," Marcus humbly thinks to himself. There was a time in Marcus' past when he became hooked on drugs. Unlike most of his family and friends, who were glad something finally knocked him down; Angelo flew to the city and offered to take Marcus back home to regroup. However Marcus chose not to leave, so Angelo stayed until Marcus got better. There are very few people Marcus would willingly give his life for, and Angelo is one of them.

Another one of God's angels that watches over Marcus besides Angelo is his grandmother, Ruth. As Marcus has gotten older, he has developed a strong bond with Ruth. Though in her nineties, Ruth, with her flowing grayish-black hair, lined with silky silver streaks, looks twenty years younger than she is. Ruth is 5'9", medium brown complexion, with a queenly essence that commands respect without her ever speaking a word. Her eyes, though piercing at times, are light brown with an outer red ring, are noticeably filled with love and knowledge that goes beyond her years. Her words of wisdom, patience and nurturing have prepared Marcus for this moment. Not to mention, her wisdom has gotten him through some of his more interesting challenges. She used to tell him "bought sense is better than none," and he never really knew what that meant. One day he was thinking about all the mistakes he had made and the lessons he learned from them, and it hit him, and all he could do was laugh. He had finally gotten it and took the time to call Ruth so she could share in his big breakthrough. "Look at her sitting there as proud as a peacock" he said to himself, "I think I'll give her a wink." He receives a smile back and the world's slowest wink.

Marcus now directs his attention to his father sitting next to his grandmother. Here sits the man who abandoned his babies, and then had no contact with them from that point on. If not for Charlie, Marcus probably wouldn't have ever spoken to him again in life. However, God has His ways and reasons and that is why Jackson is sitting on the front row as if he has been a loving and supportive father. Well, at least he came. The same can't be said about Marcus' mother. Even though he said he would pay her way, she refused to come and share in the nuptials of her only son.

Marcus stands tall in his off-white, six button long coat tuxedo, looking like a black man of distinction. His mind is racing from the past, to the present, to the future, and back to the past again. Finally, after the flower girl, ring bearer, and maid of honor have all entered and the congregation stands, he clears his mind of all thoughts except the important one, his beautiful bride. Soon she will be walking down the aisle into his arms and their new life together can begin. He tries to control and conceal his nervousness; however, his right leg starts to shake and gives him away.

"You alright man," Angelo whispers, "you're starting to turn white."

"I'm good man, but if I start to look any worse, just kick me," Marcus murmurs back. Angelo nods in agreement and pinches Marcus for good measure. "Ouch! Thanks a lot Lo."

It's 8:02 p.m.

CHAPTER II

As she watches her maid of honor start to sashay slowly down the aisle, Zephora stands behind the doors to the sanctuary with the ring bearer and flower girl, hidden from the small crowd of people and her groom, waiting to walk down the path to her destiny. This is not the wedding she always envisioned herself having. She always thought she would have an elaborate wedding with six brides' maids and a maid of honor. The church would be filled with hundreds of people all waiting to see her pass through the doors. She always thought she would be wearing a traditional wedding gown with a five foot train and two beautiful little girls holding the back of it as she walked. She always imagined her father would give her away in a church that was decorated with white and green roses on every window, at every door, and on the back of every pew, and the aisle would be lit with candles that directed her to her groom.

Zephora had found the one man that could make her smile from the inside out, which was no small feat. Because Zephora and her mother had moved around a lot when she was young, she never had a chance to make many, if any friends growing up. She never knew why they moved around all the time, just that they did. She never knew the father she dreamed would give her away, all Zephora knew was that he was dead. As a matter of fact, she didn't know of any other family besides her mother.

Zephora's mother, Saphera, has always been an excellent parent. She was very attentive to her daughter's needs. Zephora has always had the best of everything. If it had been up to Saphera, she would have had the wedding she dreamed of, except for the father giving her away part; Saphera unfortunately couldn't provide that. Saphera was an overbearing mother, but this was one time she didn't get to make any decisions about how things went.

Though they moved around all the time, Zephora and Saphera lived lives of luxury. Zephora never knew where their money came from, her mother never told her. Saphera, a woman of stature, poise and class, a queen in every sense of the word, never worked but always had a steady stream of income. Looking at Saphera, you immediately know where Zephora got her beauty; she is a shapely vanilla brown goddess who caused men to swoon in her day and still does. Saphera was furious when Zephora wouldn't let her pay for the wedding; nonetheless, Zephora and Marcus chose to pay for it themselves. They realized that marriage was about more than just the wedding day and over spending for one day did not equate to a loving marriage. Therefore, they opted for beautiful and simple which is symbolic of their relationship. Although she came from money, she did not live her life that way. Zephora had a career as a legal assistant in a prominent law firm, and her lifestyle was a reflection of that career. This both upset and confused her mother because this is not how and why she raised her daughter the way she did.

Zephora was raised to embody the characteristics of royalty and to always use proper etiquette, "sit up straight, hold your head up, roll your shoulders back when you walk, and always speak clearly and with proper English," Saphera would say. It is all Zephora had ever heard since she began to walk and talk. This was another reason why Zephora had so few friends; everyone perceived her as having an "I'm too good for you attitude," yet nothing could be further from the truth. There have only been two people who even took the time to see the person beneath the upbringing; her best friend and maid of honor, Veronica, and her soul mate and soon to be husband, Marcus.

Once Zephora finished high school, she decided to go down a different path than the one her mother had lined out for her. Saphera had the money to pay for her little African princess to go to any college in the country. Little African princess is the nickname Saphera always called Zephora, which went right along with the way she groomed her. But Zephora had a plan of her own. All she could think of was getting from under her mother's thumb. So she chose to go to a community college and learn secretarial skills. This enraged her mother. Saphera had raised her daughter to be waited on by others, not the other way around; but, she also raised her daughter to think for herself. So even though she didn't like it, she let Zephora make her own choices; however, Saphera had the power to decide when Zephora received her inheritance, the inheritance Zephora knew nothing about; and at this point, it wouldn't be anytime soon. Zephora, however, loved her work, the people she worked with and they loved her too. Her personality was only rivaled by her enchanting beauty. She had the heart of a queen; caring, loving, giving, and you could feel her spirit the moment she walked into a room. She has a glow and warmth that is matched only by her incredible smile. With her caramel skin, beautiful medium brown eyes, flowing jet black hair and curvaceous body in a five foot six inch frame; she is a vision that could have only been thought of in heaven. Even still, she never had many suitors because they viewed her as untouchable and intimidating; that is, all but one.

Standing on the other side of the sanctuary doors is her dream mate. Marcus is everything she wanted in a man. He is a man that gives his best in all he does and looks for the best in others. An entrepreneur and mentor, his character is unlike anything she had ever experienced in any other man she had ever met before. Not to mention, he is six foot one and a half inches tall with an athletic physique, a bald head with skin color that can only be described as honey chocolate brown, and a smile that is big, bold and beautiful. A strong-willed, self-made brother with a heart for helping others, whether friend or foe, he is kind, disciplined and understanding. But most of all, he loves Zephora completely; passionately and compassionately, purely and with a level of integrity that rivals that of holy men.

"I can't wait to get that man's clothes off of him and be held by his big strong hands," Zephora thinks to herself. "I didn't mind waiting for it, but I'm ready to get me some of that man right now. Umm, umm, umm, he is so fine. I hope he's ready for all this loving I've been saving up for him, because it's been a long time coming." Zephora may not be dressed in her traditional wedding gown with the long train, but she is still a vision of loveliness none the same. Her dress is egg shell white, sleeveless and form fitting with a long split in the back, covered with sequence and its length ends at a place that only allows her beautiful toes to be seen. Complementing the beauty of her dress is the gorgeous nearly flawless two karat marquise engagement ring that has two rows of three baguettes on each side that adorns her left hand. Marcus picked it out himself and totally got it right, marquise cut is her favorite.

"Thank you God for sending me this man. Please fill me with enough love and grace to keep him happy and longing for me through two lifetimes. Bless our union, Father, and allow it to be a blessing for others. As we give our best to you Father, show us how we can be better every day of our lives together. Surround us with the type of people that only embody Your beliefs. Increase us, Father, mentally, physically, spiritually, and financially for the glory of Your Kingdom and to help others' dreams come true like ours is coming true now. And Father, watch over our families and friends, and it's in Jesus Holy name I pray. Amen."

Zephora's prayer evokes a wave of goose bumps that cover her from head to toe. She smiles knowing that her words were heard by the Almighty. Now, she's ready to take the walk that will take her from her past to her future. As Veronica slowly makes her way down the aisle, Zephora starts to get nervous. "What if I'm boring? What if he gets tired of me? I'm okay. He loves me. I know he loves me. We'll be okay.

Breathe, breathe, breathe. I'm ready." And with that Zephora takes a deep breath and calms herself.

It's 8:07 p.m.

CHAPTER III

It's 8:08 p.m., and Veronica has finally finished sashaying her way to the altar. As she takes her place opposite Angelo, she looks at him and smiles flirtatiously. Angelo, one of the coolest brothers you could ever meet, smiles back and throws in a wink for good measure. The two of them have been flirting with one another since the week began. Both Angelo and Veronica are single and unattached. It would make both Marcus and Zephora extremely happy to see those two together, they are so right for one other.

Angelo has been unattached now for about a year. His last relationship ended after three years of seemingly intense pain and suffering, and a lot of consoling and convincing from Marcus. Angelo, a handsome dark brown, six foot tall, 200 pound muscular build brother, is one of the most patient and easy going people there is; however, sometimes his logic is a little off. He would rather stay in a bad relationship, than end it and start over. He has always hated starting new relationships and finds it comforting to have someone there no matter how bad things may be. Thank goodness for Marcus. He keeps Angelo on an even keel in matters of the heart.

Veronica, on the other hand, is a very self-assured woman. She is a beautiful, shapely 36-24-38, paper sack brown, five foot five inches tall sister with a good head on her shoulders. She hasn't been in a relationship for a few years now and is happy with it. Unlike most women these days, Veronica has been taking time to strengthen her relationship with God and self, instead of leaping head first into the first thing that comes her way, and then blaming the man when it doesn't work out. Since she and Zephora met three years ago at work, the two of them were instantly best friends, and have been working on their self-esteem, self-worth, and spirituality together.

"Hey Angelo," Marcus whispers, "I have it on good authority that Veronica is digging you. But you better pray on it first before you pursue because she ain't no joke."

"Thanks for the heads up, my brother, and know that I have been praying for someone, and she might just be the answer to my prayers." Angelo whispers back. Marcus is glad to hear that. He smiles, turns his eyes upward and whispers "thank you God."

Meanwhile, Veronica's little nephew Xavier, who is the ring bearer, starts his trek down the aisle wearing his first tuxedo; the four year old receives ohs and ahs from the congregation as he walks down the aisle stopping at each row of seats to make sure everyone sees him. Ruth turns to watch him take his walk, and is overcome with emotion.

"I remember when Marcus was that small," she thinks. "I can't believe my little boy is all grown up. I'm so proud of him. He bounced back from that bad ordeal a few years back, and made the best of it. He could have folded and gave up, but he didn't, he got up and got right back in the game. I wish he had known his grandfather, he would have been so proud of Marcus too. I love that boy." Tears of joy begin to stream down her face; and she pulls out a white laced handkerchief out of her purse and dabs her eyes with it.

Xavier is now half way down the aisle and enjoying the attention he is getting from the crowd. Charlie watches as he passes the front pew and takes his place next to Marcus. Marcus places his hand on Xavier's shoulder and it keeps him calm. Charlie looks at her brother and smiles. "I can't wait for him to see what I got him for a wedding present. He has wanted this for so long, it took a while, but I'm finally ready to deliver it to him. I can't wait to see the look on his face."

Tameka, Angelo's seven year old niece, is the flower girl. Before she goes through the main sanctuary doors, she turns to Zephora and says, "You look so beautiful."

Zephora replies, "Thank you baby, you do too."

And with that, Tameka walks through the doors and starts to glide to the front of the sanctuary tossing white, pink and red rose pedals on the floor along the way.

Jackson, sitting quietly next to Charlie, bows his head and begins a silent prayer. *"Dear Lord, I know I haven't talked to you much over the years, but please hear me now. I know I haven't done right by my children, and I haven't done much right in my life, but please open the hearts of my children so that they may forgive me. Forgive me for missing my baby girl's funeral all those years ago. But mostly, Lord, right now I ask, no, I beg You; please help my son be a better husband and father than me. And bless his life always. Amen."* Jackson looks up to find Marcus staring at him intently. No smile, no frown, just a long glaring gaze. Jackson smiles and gives him a thumb's up. Marcus doesn't respond; he just continues with his stare for another minute before looking away and regaining his focus.

When Tameka reaches the front and takes her place next to Veronica, tears begin to flow down Saphera's face. Here comes the bride begins to play. The congregation stands, and Saphera reaches in her purse and pulls out a tissue to wipe her eyes.

"My baby is so beautiful. She hasn't done things the way I would have, but I'm so very proud of her. I didn't even get a chance to tell her about the history of her father's people. Oh Zuri, you would be so proud of your daughter. I've kept your secrets my husband; and I will continue to do so."

Marcus gets his first glimpse of his bride and can't believe his eyes. "Cuz, pick your lip up off the floor," whispers Angelo. However, Marcus is not the only one with a dropped lip, every man, woman, and child in the congregation needed to wipe the dirt off their bottom lips too. Even Stevie Wonder could see that Zephora is the most beautiful bride to ever grace the inside of this church and a lot more as well.

As the beautiful bride stands in the entrance of the sanctuary, she is met by Veronica's father, Calvin, who is graciously waiting for her hand; for he will have the honor and pleasure of giving Zephora away. Without any men in her life to speak of, Zephora was without a male family member to give her away. Veronica, as any best friend would, offered up her father for the job, and neither he nor Zephora could be happier. The congregation stands and turns to see the beautiful bride.

While all eyes were on the bride, Angelo took a look beyond the bride and saw three gentlemen sneaking in from the left side of the sanctuary entrance. A few seconds later he spies a dapper older man slide in on the right side of the sanctuary and take a seat in the back. While everyone else is focused on the bride, including Marcus, Angelo keeps his attention on this new activity in the rear of the sanctuary as he has never seen any of these men before, and as best man and best friend, he feels it is his duty to be aware seeing that Marcus' focus is only on Zephora. Angelo doesn't want anyone or anything to mess this up for Marcus and Zephora.

As Zephora and Calvin elegantly make their way to the front of the church, the minister is anxious to begin. "Who gives this woman away, as stunning as she is?" Calvin replies, "I do, but as fine as she is, I wish I didn't have to."

The congregation bursts into uncontrollable laughter as Calvin hands Zephora off to Marcus. Now, finally, hand in hand, Marcus and Zephora glance at one another and step up to the altar and stand in front of the minister, wearing smiles so big you could easily count all their teeth and cavities. The congregation takes their seat and the ceremony is about to begin.

It's 8:25 p.m.

CHAPTER IV

"The institution of marriage should not be entered into lightly. The union of a man and a woman is the most important relationship two can enter into, besides the relationship each and every individual should have with themselves and with God Almighty. Standing here before me today are two people who realize the importance of this commitment. Partly because I told them in our premarital counseling sessions, which I encourage any of you thinking of making this commitment to attend, and partly because before they came to me, they sought God in this matter. It is not just a promise between the two of them which they enter into, but also a promise which they make separately and together with God as well. And it is for that very reason; we are having this ceremony today in front of God and in front of all you witnesses. Now, with that being said, and before I go any further, I ask all here in attendance today, if you know of any reason why these two people should not be joined as one here today, to speak now or forever hold your peace." It's 8:30 p.m., and silence falls over the entire church congregation.

Saphera closes her eyes and clinches her eyelids together so that her eyes are tightly shut. "Please Lord, please," Saphera prays to herself.

Marcus and Zephora, who are facing one another, simultaneously turn their heads to face the congregation. Zephora notices the look on her mother's face and is perplexed and bewildered by it.

"What could she be thinking that is causing her to show so much anguish on her face?" Zephora wonders. After contemplating why her mother's face is riddled with so much fear, Zephora is suddenly gripped by fear herself even though she doesn't know why. Maybe it's the fact that her mother who usually shows so little emotion now seems to be overcome with it. Whatever the reason, in that second Zephora instantly became unsure of herself and of her marriage to Marcus.

Marcus searches the crowd from right to left. He doesn't notice any crazy ex-girlfriends lurking in the corners. Then he catches site of Alisha. She and Marcus had a serious relationship that lasted a few years some time ago, but they had resolved any issues they once had and were friends now. Their eyes met and instantly he could see what she was feeling. His heart could feel the love that Alisha was displaying on her face. Marcus got a huge lump in his throat and swallows hard to clear it.

Marcus thinks to himself, "after all this time, and now she chooses this moment to show that she still has love for me? That time has come and gone Alisha, keep your mouth shut and don't get up either. Please Lord; please don't let that heifer get up." He notices tears running down her face. She breaks their eye contact by dropping her head and wiping her eyes. "Oh my God, I thought she was going to get up. I pray the right man finds her just as I found Zephora." *"Please Lord, comfort her and send the man you made for her to her. In Jesus name I pray."* Marcus' heartbeat begins to slow again as he turns to look at his bride. As he does, he notices the look of fear on her face and gently tightens the hold he has on her hand. Zephora looks up at Marcus and he stares deeply into her eyes, and rubs the top of her hands with his thumbs in an attempt to calm her fears of the moment.

It's 8:31 p.m.

Angelo looks out over the congregation and notices one of the three late comers stand to his feet. "No don't you do this," Angelo thinks to himself. Then the other two men, flanking the first man on both sides, rise as well. In a single motion, Marcus and Zephora cease their unified gaze into each other's eyes and turn their heads in the direction of the three unknown gentlemen. Little did they know that this moment signified the end to what had begun as the start to a brand new life for the bride and groom.

It's 8:32 p.m.

"Hold it!!" shouts the stranger. All heads turn in the direction of the three men who were now standing. "I am Kwazan. Leader of the ruling family of the Eastern Thulamalan tribe of Malawi a country rich in gold, diamonds, and other precious stones in southeastern Africa, and by Tribal Law this woman, Zephora, belongs to me." Saphera stands to her feet, turns toward her daughter in disbelief, and faints. Her descent to the floor happens as if she is falling in slow motion.

It's 8:34pm.

CHAPTER V

As Saphera begins to fall, Marcus jumps down from beside his bride to catch her, and manages to do so just before her head is about to hit the floor. Screams and shouts fill the sanctuary. Pastor Chappell tries hopelessly to get things under control. Kwazan makes his way through the crowd of frightened people to the front of the church, led by his two personal guardsmen who push and shove people to clear a path, and attempts to grab Zephora's hand. Instantly and instinctively, Marcus jumps up from his kneeling position and steps between Kwazan and Zephora. "Step back brother before I go off in here." Kwazan's guards immediately pull Kwazan back and step in front of him. Almost simultaneously, Angelo steps down and stands to the right of Marcus.

"Do we have a problem?" Angelo asks. Marcus glances at Angelo and smiles. Instantaneously he is reminded of a time long ago when he and Angelo stood side by side like this against six guys. It wasn't Angelo's fight then either; however, just like this moment, Angelo came charging in to help.

"Just like old times Lo?" Marcus responds. "Yup, just like old times. Sorry about your wedding getting crashed,"

Angelo remarks. "Just a snag brother, just a snag," replies Marcus. "Marcus!" Zephora screams out.

In his haste to protect Zephora, Marcus let Saphera go and her head bounced hard against the floor. Zephora rushes over to her, but she is out cold. Charlie jumps up to protect her brother; however, Jackson pulls her back down. "Calm down girl, he can handle this," Jackson confidently states. "Charlie be cool and take care of Granny, I got this," Marcus says calmly.

Marcus glances over the entire room and perceives the people getting agitated with the situation, and some of them are starting to move toward the front. The situation is becoming volatile as members of the congregation begin pointing fingers and yelling at Kwazan. One of his guards turns his back to Marcus and Angelo to turn and face the crowd. The guards' moods become hostile and they begin to reach in their coats for their weapons.

"Everyone, stop and calm down please!" yells Marcus. The place becomes dead quiet. So quiet, you could hear a pin drop. "Now, please, please, everyone clear the sanctuary," Marcus firmly states, "and someone call an ambulance." "You," Marcus points at Kwazan, "please, take a seat over here." Marcus has taken control of the situation, and everyone follows his commands.

Zephora, who has tears streaming down her face and is gently stroking her mother's head, looks up at Marcus, smiles tenderly, and thinks to herself, "I love that man. The way he takes charge turns me on. Curse this Kwamy guy, I should be having my first dance as Mrs. Marcus Howard; but no, he gotta come in here and screw up my day with this madness. I am not his woman, that man done lost his ever loving mind. I wonder what in the hell he is talking about. I belong to Marcus, mind, soul, and especially body."

When the ambulance arrives, they quickly tend to Saphera. As they roll her out on the stretcher, Marcus stands up and takes charge again.

"Kwazan," Marcus sternly addresses him, "we are going to the hospital. You're welcome to come along; better yet, I insist you come along and explain what in God's name you are talking about. Angelo can you and Veronica tend to things here and meet us at the hospital afterwards?" "I got you brother," Angelo replies.

Hand in hand Marcus and Zephora follow the paramedics out of the church and get in Marcus' car together.

Marcus' family prepares to follow them. Kwazan and his men get into their limo, and the rest of the people slowly disperse in utter dismay at the evenings suspense filled turn of events. As the last of the cars leave, the older gentleman who was the last one to enter the church is now the last one to exit it. As he slides through the doors, Pastor Chappell pushes them open and waves to the gentleman as he gets into the back of a black Crown Victoria with dark tinted windows, an obvious unmarked government car.

As they are driving to the hospital, Marcus and Zephora are finally alone and get a chance to talk about the turn of events. "Who in the hell is this Kwazan dude and where did he come from?" Marcus asks.

"I don't know baby, I've never seen him before in my life," Zephora answers. "Well, from the look your mother gave you before she fainted, I would have to say she knows something," insists Marcus. "When she wakes up, we can ask her, but I can't imagine how she knows this guy from middle Africa," Zephora explains.

"She had better have some good answers to why we ain't married and happily on our way to our honeymoon suite," Marcus remarks.

"I second that baby, but we could already have the answer if you hadn't let her head bounce off that concrete floor," Zephora quips.

"Oops, my bad; but I couldn't let that dude put his hands on you. You're my lady and my first priority," Marcus declares.

Zephora leans over to kiss Marcus on the cheek and gives him a sultry sexy smile that does its intended job and sends fire all the way to Marcus' loins. "Alright, don't start none, won't be none; we are not married yet," Marcus responds.

Meanwhile, in Kwazan's limo, a different conversation is going on. "Wasn't she exquisite?" Kwazan asks.

"Yes sir."

"A vision of pure loveliness," Kwazan asserts.

"Yes sir."

"We must do something about this guy of hers or she will never be mine," insists Kwazan.

"Do you want us to take him out?" asks one of his guards.

"No, not yet; he is not a threat now, but get someone to watch him," demands Kwazan.

"Yes sir, right away."

"I think once he knows the deal and understands the situation, he will not be any more trouble."

Meanwhile in the unmarked government car, another set of plans are being made.

"Agent Garret?" says the older gentleman.

"Yes sir."

"Get a couple of guys to keep an eye on Marcus."

"Yes sir."

"And get two more men to protect Saphera and Zephora."

Yes sir."

"No contact, just keep a close eye on them, all of them," orders the older gentleman.

"Yes sir; and what about the wedding crashers," asks agent Garret.

"Well, as for this Kwazan character, get the local police to stop his limo once he leaves the hospital and check his credentials. Let's find out who he really is," replies the older gentleman.

"Yes sir."

As Saphera is brought into the ER, Marcus and Zephora sign her in, and everyone else who chose to tag along settles into the waiting area. The ER doctor explains to Zephora and Marcus that Saphera has a serious concussion.

"We have her sedated because of her rapid heartbeat. She will be resting for a while, and we want to keep her here overnight for observation," states the ER doctor.

"Thanks doctor; when she comes to, please let us know?" Zephora replies.

"No problem."

"Okay baby, she's going to be out for a while, so let's go and talk to this nut-case who crashed our wedding," Marcus demands.

"Marcus honey, I would rather talk to my mother first," insists Zephora.

"Not a chance, I want to hear what this guy has to say for himself," states Marcus.

"If you say so honey," Zephora responds in duress.

As they walk hand in hand to the waiting area, both their minds are racing trying to figure out what is going on. All Zephora can think about is running away with her man and getting away from all this madness. While Marcus, on the other hand, is ready to solve all this guy's problems the old fashion way for ruining his wedding and hurting the feelings of his betrothed. However, he knows that nothing will be right in his world until he gets to the bottom of this marriage crashing thing, so he settles himself and prepares to sit down and be civil about it. The quicker he gets answers, the sooner he can get back to marrying Zephora, the woman of his dreams.

PART 2

LOVE OR THE LAW

CHAPTER VI

As they approach the waiting area, Marcus tries his best to assure Zephora that everything will be alright. She is so nervous that her hands are shaking and sweating, and she begins to rub them together in an attempt to evaporate the moisture. Marcus' family, Angelo, Veronica, Calvin and the kids are all sitting in the waiting area with anticipation. On the other side of the room sits Kwazan and his men patiently waiting the arrival of Marcus and Zephora.

"Hey Angelo," says Veronica. "What the hell is going on?"

"Well, Zephora's mom hit her head," Angelo chimes in.

"I know that silly. I'm talking about with this other guy," Veronica quips back.

"I'm not sure yet, but I can't wait to find out. Do you need anything Veronica, maybe some coffee?" Angelo asks with concern.

"No, I'm fine, but thanks for asking. You're always such a gentleman," Veronica responds while batting her eyes.

"Yeah, we are a dying breed. Hopefully, when this is all over, maybe you'll allow me to take you out and show you more of what a gentleman is all about," Angelo suggests.

"You know what, Angelo, Veronica charmingly states, I was beginning to think that you would never ask. I would love to go out with you."

Angelo smiles intently and sits back in his chair and places his arm around Veronica. She responds by moving in a little closer. The two of them settle in for the long haul as Veronica leans in closer and puts her head on Angelo's shoulder.

Charlie's knees are shaking with anxiety. Jackson puts his hand on her right knee to stop the shaking.

"I wish I knew what was going on Daddy," Charlie says.

"Yeah, me too, however, if I know anything about your brother, he can handle this guy and whatever he has to say," Jackson assures.

"I hope this is just some big mistake, because I really like Zephora," Charlie responds. "And she's so perfect for Marcus. She's the only woman I have ever seen handle him so well, and still allow him to be himself."

"Is that your professional opinion," Jackson retorts.

"It's just the truth. She allows him to be the man he is, and then adds a sense of balance without taking anything away from her own essence as a woman. She's my Shero," Charlie insists.

"Sounds like your mother when I first met her. She was an incredible woman. I was just not man enough to handle her," Jackson admits. As he finishes his sentence, Jackson puts his head in his hands and lowers it. However, Charlie won't let him off the hook that easy.

"Not only were you not man enough, but you also succeeded in driving her crazy to the extent that she abused her own children because they reminded her of your crazy ass," Charlie scowls. And with that, she gets up and walks toward her little brother who is slowly approaching the waiting area.

"Marcus, what's going on and how's Saphera?"

"She's fine and resting now. I'll find out what's up with this dude in a few minutes."

"Zephora, do you know this guy?" Charlie asks.

"Listen Sis," Marcus scowls. "Let us handle our business, and as soon as we know something, we will fill everyone in."

"Okay, but you don't have to snap at me," Charlie shouts.

"My bad Sis, but you know the deal," Marcus relents.

Marcus, for the most part, is doing a good job of remaining calm in the middle of all the drama. Even though they didn't get married, Marcus and Zephora look like the perfect couple who love and support one another; and that love is truly being tested. And now sitting in front of Kwazan, they are about to get some answers.

"How is your mother?" Kwazan asks.

"She'll be fine, she's resting," responds Zephora.

Then Kwazan, with the politeness of royalty replies, "And how are you my beautiful queen?"

"Hold up partner!" Marcus interjects. "Stop addressing my lady as your queen and talk to me. I'm the one you owe an explanation to. So, before you say another word to Zephora, you need to let me know why you so rudely interrupted our wedding."

"My apology friend, I mean no disrespect. I was just being polite. I know this must be confusing and very frustrating for you, however, when I am finished you will realize that she is my queen and you will let her go," ,Kwazan rebuts with confidence.

At that moment, Zephora jumps up and starts shouting. "Stop jaw jacking and get to it, I'm losing my patience!"

"Calm down baby, I got it," Marcus assures and then turns to address the interloper. "Okay, Kwazan, let's hear it."

"Fine, please listen carefully to the story I will tell you and afterwards, I will show you the proof of my claims," Kwazan replies with a hint of agitation in his voice. Sensing he finally has everyone's attention; Kwazan, with a deep alluring South African accent, begins to tell his story and that of his people.

"A thousand years ago a group of people who were from the very southern tip of Africa, traveled north to the eastern quadrant of Africa. These are the people that founded the great city called Mapungubwe."

"Oh," Zephora exclaims, "the City of Gold. My mother told me about it."

"I am sure she did, since they are your people too," Kwazan responds.

"Excuse me," exclaims Zephora.

"That is right you are a direct descendant of the people of Mapungubwe. Now, these people, your people, are very important and special because they represent one of the first great kingdoms of southern Africa. They also had one of the first political structures and separation of social class in the region. For three hundred and fifty years the city thrived and prospered. Because of the city's location, it was in the middle of the east coast trading lane. The Mapungubwean people traded gold, copper and jewels with China and India. They also raised livestock and farmed. Their political structure consisted of five noble families who transferred the leadership of the nation from one family to the next every century. When they abandoned their city, they left very little behind, thus giving the appearance to the outside world that they had no written language or civility.

Interestingly enough, during this same period of time, across the northern border of what is now South Africa and into what is now Zimbabwe, there was another set of people thriving in another one of Africa's great cities, The Great Zimbabwe. Like the city of Mapungubwe, they also had political and social structure. Also interesting is the fact that there structures were nearly the same. It was taught to us that at one time or another, the two people were in fact one. The Great Zimbabwe was also part of the eastern trade lane, and also traded their goods and services with other countries. This is our history.

"Our history, what do you mean, our history?" responds Zephora.

"Our history shows that the two cities traded with one another. And I say our history because the people of The Great Zimbabwe are my ancestors."

"Well, that is a great story," blurts out Marcus, "but it still doesn't explain why you had the audacity to interrupt my wedding, and I'm getting pretty tired of it quite frankly, so get to the point, because up to this point, both Zephora and I know the history of these two great cities. In fact, we even know that white people have been downplaying their very existence since they first discovered the cities. They even tried to erase parts of what they found. Their arrogance would not let them believe that people indigenous to South Africa could have ever built anything as incredible as what they found without the help of some foreign power. However, let's get back to how this affects me and Zephora."

"How do you know of these things?" Kwazan asks.

"Just because we live in America doesn't mean we don't know African history. We, and when I say we, I mean all black Americans, are part of that history as well. And even though the white people of this country have tried their best to keep us from knowing any part of that history, some of us strive to learn about it anyway. Now get back to the point," Marcus responds.

Meanwhile, slipping in the back door of the hospital, the men from the government car make their way to Saphera's room.

"You two stand guard out here; I will only be a minute."

"Yes Sir Mr. Netumba."

CHAPTER VII

Now in Saphera's room, Mr. Netumba walks over and places his hand on her forehead and rubs gently between her eyebrows with his thumb.

"Oh Saphera, you are still so beautiful and Zephora is even more beautiful than I could have ever imagined. Sorry you have to go through all of this mess, but it will all be over soon." As Mr. Netumba removes his hand from Saphera's head, she starts to come around. She is noticeably groggy, and her vision is blurry. As she opens her eyes, she is able to make out a figure standing over her.

"Uh, what happened? Who's there? Zuri is that you? How are you here? I've missed you so much. Zuri come and talk to me." Mr. Netumba steps back and slips back out the door. Saphera falls back asleep with a smile on her face thinking she just saw her late husband.

Zuri, Saphera's late husband, was killed in a car accident. His car went over a cliff and exploded, and because the car was completely burned, his body was never recovered. He was an extremely wealthy man and he left Saphera and Zephora very well off. They actually have enough money to last for several generations.

Mr. Netumba and his team leave Saphera's room and try to slip back out of the hospital unseen by anyone. They almost made it, but Charlie spotted them leaving Saphera's room while she was walking the halls trying to avoid Jackson after their episode.

"Who are you and why were you in Saphera's room?" Shouts Charlie.

"Excuse me."

"You heard me. Why were you in there and who are you?"

"Listen Charlie."

"How do you know my name and who in the hell are you?!"

"If you would calm down a second, I'll tell you. Gentlemen will you please escort her outside so we can talk."

"Don't touch me!"

"Listen Ms. Howard, you see this federal badge? It says I can take you anywhere I want. Now calm down, and come along with us quietly, I have a few questions for you."

"Look Mister, I haven't done anything, so you really have no right to touch me. So like I said, take your hands off me boy!"

"Ms. Howard, don't you want to help your brother Marcus?"

"What the hell are you talking about, and how do you know my brother?"

"Calm down and come with us and I'll tell you all about it. You know, you really should feel good about yourself."

"And why is that?"

"Because the wedding gift you got your brother is perfect and he's going to love it. Trust me."

"Who in the hell are you and how do you know what I got my brother for his wedding? What branch of the government do you work for?

"I didn't say but it has to do with foreign policy and international security measures."

Okay, I'll go with you, but you need to start answering some of my questions."

"All in due time Ms. Howard, all in due time."

"Let me go and tell my family that I'm leaving with you."

"No, wait! You can't tell them about us. You can only talk to your grandmother. Tell her that you have to get away from Jackson, so you're taking a cab back to your room."

"How do you know about Jackson?

"I know about your entire family. They're just not ready to know about me yet."

"What! Who in the hell are you?"

"Listen Ms. Howard, please do not say or do anything that will make me regret letting you do this. National security is at stake."

"Okay, okay, I'll be right back."

"My man here will be watching you, so please do as I say."

"Okay, I got it." As Charlie walks away with her chaperone to let Ruth know she is leaving, Mr. Netumba shakes his head in disbelief at the turn of events.

"I hope I won't be sorry for this later."

"Me too sir. She could be a problem."

"I don't think so, or I hope not. I think she will do anything to protect her brother. At least, that's what I'm counting on. She has already done more than she realizes. We just have to get her to play things our way."

"Yes sir, Mr. Netumba."

Now back in the waiting area, Charlie rolls her eyes at Jackson and takes a seat next to her grandmother. "Granny, I need to get out of here, daddy is getting on my nerves. So, I'm taking a cab back to the hotel. Can you let Marcus know?"

"How am I going to get back?"

"Daddy will take you."

"Okay baby, but don't think of me as no fool."

"Whatcha talking about granny?"

"Charlie, don't you never mind. You just go ahead, I'll be alright. Just remember your old grandmother ain't no fool. I see what everybody think I don't see. But you go, I'll be alright. I just hope you know what you're doing."

"I do granny. I'll be okay. Bye."

"Bye baby."

Mr. Netumba's man watches from the corridor seemingly unnoticed. Charlie makes her way back to the hall and they walk away together to meet up with Mr. Netumba. They leave the hospital through the back and get into the unmarked government car. "So, where are we going?" Charlie asks. "I'm taking a big chance trusting you."

"There's a Waffle House down the street. I was thinking we could go there and talk."

"Sure that's fine. I can't wait to hear what you've got to say, plus, I'm hungry."

Back at the hospital, Dr. Jones comes out to let Zephora and Marcus know that Saphera is coming around. "Can we see her?" requests Zephora.

"Absolutely, she's asking for you. But only one at a time, please."

"I'll go Marcus. Will you be okay?"

"Sure honey. I'll keep trying to get the truth out of this guy. Give your mother my love."

"Okay baby. I'll be back. Love ya."

"Love you, too." Just then, Ruth walks up to Marcus and taps him on the shoulder.

"Excuse me Marcus."

"Yes granny."

"Baby I'm ready to go. Did this fella tell you anything yet?"

"No granny. Not yet. But I think I'm getting close to something."

"I'm gonna get your father to take me to the hotel. I need to rest. Your sister already left. She said she was taking a cab. When you find out what's going on, you call me. But son, remember this – God don't make no mistakes. If He said that girl is your wife, and I believe He did, then she will be. Maybe there is something God wants you to know, needs you to know. Now you listen carefully to whatever this man has to say, but you must trust God no matter what happens. He is in control of all things. And no matter what happens, all things work for the good for those who love God. Now I gotta go, I love you baby and I'll see you in the morning. Just trust God baby, trust God."

"Yes Ma'am. Thank you. I love you so much. I'll go get Pop to take you to the hotel." Marcus goes over to his father, who is nodding in his chair and asks him to take Ruth to the hotel. Jackson yawns and stretches and slowly gets up to do his appointed task.

"Son, I don't know what's going on here, and I know I haven't been there for you in the past, but I'm here now for whatever you need."

"Thanks Pop. Please just take granny to the hotel.

"I will, but you just remember - trust God son, trust God."

"That's funny; granny just said the same thing."

"Confirmation son, confirmation; no matter what happens, just remember that."

"She said that, too. What do ya'll know that I don't?"

"Son, I told you, trust God. Everyone in this world has the potential to let you down, but if you trust God, He will never let you down. Do your part son, and God is faithful to do His. God can do anything, except fail."

CHAPTER VIII

Jackson and Ruth leave the hospital and take the journey back to the hotel. As they are driving, Ruth turns her head and looks out of her window just in time to see her granddaughter sitting in the Waffle House restaurant talking with three men. She doesn't say anything to Jackson; she just turns her head back forward and smiles. Ruth knows that Charlie had to have had a good reason to lie to her because she rarely ever risks telling her one. Ruth also knows that something is not quite right about all of this, but at ninety, she is much too old to interfere in the matters of these young folk. Jackson looks over and notices Ruth smiling. He is curious as to what she has to be smiling about after such a disastrous day. "What is it that you are smiling about over there?"

"Oh nothing Jackson, I'm just ready to get back home.

Jackson doesn't pry, he knows better. Ruth has just recently started warming up to him. She has never really liked him from the first time she met him. As far as she is concerned, he is the reason her daughter is a little off now. Jackson was the first boy Esther ever showed an interest in. It was back when Esther was a junior in high school and Jackson was a senior. Ruth had a feeling he was going to be bad news, so she wouldn't allow Esther to see him.

When Jackson graduated, he left and went off to college, and Ruth figured that would be the end of it. However, Esther got accepted to the same college that Jackson was attending, and once she got there, their romance blossomed. After Esther's first year of college, she became pregnant and dropped out, and the rest, as they say, is history. After years of a rocky and abusive marriage, she left and Jackson followed only to decide later that a wife and kids was cramping his style, hence, the bad blood between him and Ruth.

Zephora enters Saphera's room and is surprised to see her mother sitting up and smiling. She expected her to be doped up and groggy. However, Saphera was wide awake and ready to talk. "Zephora honey, I saw your father!"

"Now mother, you know that's impossible. Father died a long time ago, right?"

"Yes. I don't know, but he was here. I saw him."

"Okay mother, just calm down. You know you hit your head awfully hard. You could have been dreaming."

"I wasn't dreaming Zephora."

Zephora decided to indulge her mother. "Well, did he talk to you?"

"No, he didn't talk to me, but that's not the point. The point is I saw him, which means he's alive. You know they never found his body."

"Mother! The car exploded and was burned to a crisp. They didn't find his body because there wasn't anything left to find."

"Never mind that baby. More importantly, I have something to tell you."

"I hope so because some guy I've never met before and didn't care to ever meet, just ruined my special day. So yeah, you need to have something to tell me."

Saphera can hear in Zephora's voice that she is highly upset and that she needs to come clean. She thought she would never have to reveal the truth, never thought this day would come. She tells her daughter to pull a chair over to the bed and listen closely to what she has to say. Zephora reluctantly takes a seat and agrees to listen. She knows she has no choice if she ever wants to find out what's really going on.

Saphera begins by telling Zephora that she loves her and that she is the most important person in her life. "You are the descendant of a long line of kings and queens. Your ancestors were one of the first great people of the Southern African region, and you are the last remaining member of your family and an heiress."

"An heiress to what?"

"Your grandfather, before he was killed and your father signed a document that officially and legally binds you to the son of one of southern Africa's wealthiest and most influential families."

"Why didn't you ever tell me this before? Why did you sit back and allow me to date and fall in love with Marcus. Why mother, why would you do that?"

"Honestly? I thought it would never come up. Your grandfather was killed by a rival family from his tribe, and I believed, until today, that your father was too. So I didn't think there was a point. Listen, when we first met, your father told me this incredible tale about ancient tribes and a tribal law. I thought he just had a big imagination and it was part of his rap to me. I thought it was cute. Well, we fell in love and got married. Afterwards, he took me to his bank, showed me that he was worth a fortune and then took me in the vault. There he opened a safety deposit box, and in it were some very old laminated scrolls that were written in some ancient African language."

"He explained to me that they were the official seven hundred year old records of his people in their original form. They bind his family to the family of some other tribe forever. He told me it was my job to keep these records safe. He also told me of a rival family from his tribe that wanted to replace their family in the legacy of this tribal law. This is the reason that his family ended up here in the United States. Because of the influence this rival family had in the council with the other royal families, they all conspired against your family. Their plan was to kill all the members of your ancient family; however, your ancestors got wind of this plot. So they gathered all their belongings and their wealth, which consisted of millions maybe even billions of dollars' worth of gold, diamonds and precious jewels and fled. But not before they retrieved official scrolls of the tribes' history and of the plot to oust them from the tribes' record keeper. All the scrolls bear the official tribe seal.

Unfortunately, it didn't end there. Tribal assassins were dispatched to find and eliminate every member of your family. Your father and grandfather were able to dodge these assassins for years. Your father told me that one day some men approached him and your grandfather. The men were representatives of the family from the other tribe that they were bound to. They explained that they knew about the assassins and were there to help. They told them that they could put an end to it all; however, your father had to sign documents that bound his children to their children just as it bound the families of their ancestors long ago. Your father agreed, however, two weeks later your grandfather was killed.

After we got married, your father was sure someone was still out to get him. That is why we split up the minute we knew I was pregnant with you. And, that's why we always moved around. When your father was killed, I thought it was over. I didn't know anyone knew about us. I kept my maiden name of Sherman and thought we were in the clear. But, apparently not; they were watching us, and maybe watching over us, all this time."

"You know Mother, that's a great story, one for the archives. However, it is one that maybe I should have known about years ago. You make me want to cuss; the fact that you have been withholding this information from me is unbelievable. All this time I thought we had an open relationship, an honest relationship, but now, I see that was not the case at all." Zephora shakes her head in disbelief. "So what else are you not telling me? Do I have a brother or sister that I don't know about? Lies destroy relationships all the time and a lie of omission is still a lie."

"No baby you don't and I have told you everything I know. I'm sorry I didn't tell you, but I thought I was doing what was best for you, best for us."

"Yeah, whatever Mother. You have single-handedly ruined my life, the life you say you were trying to protect. I was about to marry the man of my dreams and your lies ruined it, ruined my life! So tell me Mother, what is my family name, the name of my Father and his people that you have been hiding from me all my life?"

"It's Netumba."

CHAPTER IX

Meanwhile, back in the waiting area, as Kwazan continues his story, Marcus is starting to get a little impatient, however, he remains composed. Kwazan proceeds to tell how the people of Mapungubwe and his people, the people of the Great Zimbabwe, begin to notice a change in the trading lanes. The area was beginning to be saturated with whites. The leaders of the two great cities met to decide their fate. The leaders of both cities agreed and decided it would be prudent to relocate their respective people. They decided to move their people further north to avoid the rash of whites that were entering and settling in the country.

The time stamp was the early fifteenth century. The two people migrated to the northeast. The people of Great Zimbabwe stopped first and settled some two hundred miles away from their original city. The people of Mapungubwe continued on another hundred miles or so making their journey a total of about three hundred seventy five miles.

Marcus is getting irritated and stops Kwazan from talking. "Listen brother that all sounds very interesting, but you need to be getting to the point. You have been doing a lot of talking and yet I am no closer to any answers now than when you started, and my patience is wearing thin.

"I am getting to the point of interest to you now. Just please allow me to finish."

"Just get to it man."

"Each group of people settled in rich and fertile lands. The Zimbabwe people, my people, settled in a land that was rich in gold ore and fertile for farming. In addition, we also found small amounts of diamonds and other precious stones. The people of Mapungubwe settled in a land that was rich in diamonds, precious jewels, land that was fertile for farming, and some traces of gold ore. In the sixteenth century, the leaders of both these great people met and decided that because of their rich lands they wanted to have lasting peace between one another. To achieve this, they implemented an ordinance they called Tribal Law.

The basis of this law reduced the leadership core of each people to four instead of five families. Each family of each tribe would rule their respective people for a century and then step down for the next family in line to take its rightful place. The firstborn son of the ruling family of one tribe was to be promised to the firstborn daughter of the other tribe, or vice versa, to ensure lasting peace. Members of each noble family of each tribe sat on the leadership council of both tribes. These laws along with some others have been in place for centuries and are still in place today.

Zephora is the first born of her father and a descendant of this century's ruling family from her tribe. I am the first born of my father and descendant of this century's ruling family from my tribe. So by Tribal Law she is to be my wife."

"Man, you got to be kidding me; all of this because of some ancient African law? You stopped and ruined my wedding for some law that has nothing to do with us here in America?"

"On the contrary Brother Marcus, even the width and depth of the Atlantic Ocean cannot break the binding power of our Tribal Law."

"Man what in the hell are you talking about? There is no way you can enforce that mess here. And if you try, I will see you in court."

"There is no need for that, I brought proof."

"What Proof?"

"I have here a contract signed by my father and Zephora's father that binds us together in marriage as the first born children of the ruling families of our respective tribes for this century."

"Zephora's father is dead, and dead men don't sign contracts," Marcus retorts.

"This contract was signed thirty days after I was born and before Zephora was born. Her mother knows this to be true."

"How is it that Zephora's family ended up here in America?"

"That is an interesting story in itself. A few centuries back, one of Zephora's ancestors stumbled on an illegal change in the ancient scrolls that was approved by six of the eight governing families. Once those six families found out her ancestor knew about the change, they ordered her entire family to be assassinated. When the word got back to her ancestors, they took their accumulated wealth and fled the country, and somehow they ended up here. However, the assassins pursued them and were thought to have completed their task. Some years back it was learned that members of the family had survived and another assassin was dispatched. When my father found out about the new contract of assassination, he ordered a council meeting and decreed that the assassinations come to a halt because it was a breach of our laws. All the leaders agreed, however, they were unable to contact the assassin. My father sent men to protect Zephora's remaining family but the assassin was able to get to both her father and grandfather. Fortunately, her father had the wisdom to keep his distance from his wife and child which kept them safe."

"So are these assassins still out there?"

"No, we were able to eliminate them. So you see Zephora is to be my wife. Your claim on her doe not matter. I am sorry you had to find out this way, but it is over, she belongs to me."

"Kwazan let me tell you something. Before I loose Zephora, we will surely end up in court. You see, unlike you, my hold on her is based on love and not some supposed signed contract. You don't know her or anything about her. I, on the other hand, know everything about her. So do me a favor and leave. When she comes back, you won't be here. Give me a number where you can be reached and I'll have my attorney call you."

"Okay Marcus, I will leave, but this will not dismiss my claim. In the end you will see that I am right. Within the next three months, she will be my wife whether you like it or not, and whether she likes it or not. It is for the greater good. My people need her. Her people need her. And without her and without this marriage they will be in chaos. The Tribal Law of our people is that powerful, that honored, and supersedes any other law in my country."

"Unfortunately for you and your people Kwazan, she is needed here too. And we honor something more powerful than your Tribal Law – and that's our Love. And there is nothing more powerful in this world and in this universe than love."

CHAPTER X

Angelo and Veronica are a couple of great friends. They have been patiently waiting for their respective best friends at the hospital, even though it is New Year's Eve. They noticed Kwazan and his crew leaving and rushed over to Marcus to get all the details. However, one good thing did come out of all of this madness, and that's the time Angelo and Veronica got to spend together while waiting. They exchanged their information, set dates for the New Year and have a mutual affection for one another growing.

As they approach Marcus, they notice the discouraging look on his face and decided it would be best to talk to him together.

"Look at him Angelo, he looks so bewildered. He's your best friend, so I'll just hang back while you find out what's going on."

"Gee thanks Veronica. Thought we decided we were in this together? You big chicken," Veronica shrugs her shoulders, bats her big brown eyes at Angelo, and gives him her cute little girl smile. He shakes his head and continues on toward Marcus.

"Okay Marcus, what's the deal? Did you tell that trifling Negro to get to stepping so you can get married?" Angelo tried to lighten the moment with his candor, however, the look on Marcus' face and his body language said he wasn't in the mood.

As Marcus' and Angelo's eyes meet, instantly, Angelo knows that things are not going to be as cut and dry as they had all hoped. Even Veronica, watching from the distance, could tell that the situation had taken a turn for the worst. Marcus somehow is always able to find the silver lining in any dark cloud, holds his head high and is still able to muster up a smile as he extends his hand towards Angelo's to give him some dap.

"Well brother, he put his cards on the table, and I gotta tell ya, it's a pretty good hand. Couple of kings, couple of queens, and I'm still waiting on him to turn over his fifth card."

"Yeah, but your hand has got to be looking pretty strong too."

"My hand, my hand right now is looking like a royal flush, but that fifth card could make me or break me."

"Okay Marcus, now I need details."

"Kwazan says he is royalty from an African tribe in Zimbabwe and that Zephora is royalty from a tribe of ancient southern African descent and because of some sixth century old Tribal Law, they are to be married."

"Get the heck out of here!"

"But wait, it gets better. He actually showed me proof in the form of a contract signed by his father and by Zephora's dead father about thirty years ago, supposedly before her father was killed."

"Was it a copy or was it an original?"

"It looked like an original."

"So, now what?"

"When Zephora gets back from seeing what her mother has to say about all of this, we will discuss it and on Monday I'll get with my attorney, and see if we can figure this mess out."

"What can I do? You know I'll make this fool disappear."

"Nothing man. Thanks, but I think I'll handle this one."

Veronica takes the time to slip down the hall to Saphera's room to be with her friend, and of course get the low down from her girl. When she gets there, she finds Saphera resting peacefully and Zephora sitting in a chair in the corner about to snap her neck from nodding. "Girl wake up before you break your neck."

Zephora is startled and jumps up in mid snore. "What, what happened?!"

"Wake up girl and tell me what the hell is going on. How you gonna leave me out there all uninformed and worried? Plus, your man is not looking to happy right now either."

"I take it Kwazan is gone?"

"Yeah, now stop stalling."

"You want the long version or the cliff notes version?"

"I just want to know what in the hell is going on." Veronica is getting impatient, not that she had a lot of patience to begin with. She and Zephora walk out into the hall to keep from waking up Saphera. She gives Zephora a raised eye, twisted mouth look and taps her foot on the floor. "I'm waiting girl."

"Well, apparently, the man I fell in love with and know is the man God made for me, is not the man I'm supposed to marry. And it's all because of the Tribal Law that my family has been a part of for centuries. And, Kwazan is who I am supposed to marry according to this law and, to keep peace between the two peoples in Africa. Now how's that for something new on your wedding day?"

"Damn girl! This fool couldn't have caught up to you with this mess before today? I don't understand that at all. And how come your Mother didn't let you know all of this before now?"

"I don't know, but I wish she had told me long before now and saved me all this heart ache."

"So who we gotta kill to make this all go away? You know I'll do it."

"Thanks Veronica, but me and Marcus gotta handle this one."

"Okay, but you know, for you, I ride and die."

PART 3

HAPPY NEW YEAR

CHAPTER XI

It's 11:58 p.m., and Marcus, Zephora, Angelo, and Veronica are all standing together in the family waiting area of the hospital. Its two minutes before the New Year and the four friends are holding hands in a circle awaiting the final two ticks of the clock. Marcus' mind is racing trying to grasp all the day has brought. This morning he just knew that at this moment he would be in the honeymoon suite in bed embracing his wife and giving her the first kiss of the New Year and of their new life together, but fate has played a nasty trick on him and flipped the script.

Zephora squeezes Marcus' hand and tries, to no avail, to hold back the tears. How could her day, her special day go so wrong? Why is this happening to her? And what can she do to change it. She begins to cry and the four of them enter into a group hug to comfort her. The toll of the day had finally started to sink in and it is more than she can stand. On top of having her wedding ruined, she has to deal with her mother, whom she has always trusted, for not disclosing her heritage to her. In her mind, her mother is ultimately to blame for the pain and anguish she is feeling now.

Everything the day handed out wasn't all bad, however. The events of the day are to blame for the sparks that are flying between Angelo and Veronica. The time they spent together this evening has given them the opportunity to make plans for the fast approaching New Year. Though they are saddened by the way things are turning out for their friends, they are also grateful to them for bringing them together.

Down the street at the Waffle house, Charlie and Mr. Netumba are toasting their good fortune over a cup of coffee. They have spent the evening exchanging notes on the situation and have come to an agreement that they need one another. Mr. Netumba has made plans to take Charlie to the Bahamas and she has agreed and is thoroughly excited about it. He has sworn her to secrecy. She can tell no one his name, or about what they have discussed. It's a tall order for Charlie because she has always had a problem keeping secrets, especially from her beloved brother Marcus.

Jackson and Ruth are back at the hotel and both are settled in, and in bed. They have been around long enough to not care about the entrance of the New Year. For them, waking up will surely be enough.

Kwazan and his team are back at their five star hotel. Kwazan is now with his aides and they are celebrating the success of their mission. According to the contract, Zephora has three months to marry him and take her place as his queen. He is feeling extremely confident because all his ducks are in a row and there is no one who has any information to refute his claim.

As the clock strikes 12:00 a.m., Marcus and his friends take the time to sing and praise God for allowing them to see another new year. Despite the awful turn of events, Marcus and Zephora are still able to thank God for His love, grace, mercy, joy, and for the love God put in their hearts for one another. They know that He is still in control of all things. The four of them take turns praying, starting with Angelo. One after the other they give thanks and pray from their hearts, for their hopes, and about their questions. They pray for peace and comfort, for love and joy, not just for themselves, but for their families and friends, the sick and shut in, the poor and disenfranchised, the powerful and the powerless, the homeless and hungry, the orphaned children, the elderly and for the entire world.

Marcus is the last to pray and when he is done, he embraces Zephora and holds her tight. He kisses her on the forehead and tells her "God said that you are my wife. He said that He made you just for me. So until He says differently, you are still mine." Then he softly presses his lips against hers. Zephora begins to smile with her heart first and then with her face because of the hope Marcus has planted inside of her. He always knows exactly what to say to comfort her. Angelo and Veronica share a hug and then their first kiss.

Marcus steps back and says to his friends, "What we share cannot be destroyed in this life or in death. Our friendship is destined; it can and will withstand all opposition. So, I say to you all; have faith, I love you, and Happy New Year!"

CHAPTER XII

Marcus rolls over and checks his clock. It's 6am and unfortunately he is in bed alone. He has only been asleep about three hours. After he took Zephora home, he decided to take the long way back to his place. Driving and listening to music always helps to clear his head. Even though it was early, he decided to get up anyway. Marcus had a routine he usually followed after he got out of bed. He would start with visiting the water closet. Then brush his teeth and shave his head. He would follow that up with a shower and then all the little grooming techniques that leaves him looking his very best. However, this morning after his shower, he just stood in front of the mirror and dried himself while looking at the floor. He held his head up, looked in the mirror, and stared at himself right in the eyes and that is when it finally hit him and he crashed.

"Why does everything have to be so difficult for me, never a simple solution to anything? Always struggling, always obstacles and giant walls to climb; import/export business – struggle. Family – major struggle. And now this; just once I would like to have something not be so damn hard. I tell you God, you got me wondering if you really like me at all. You tell me that she's my wife only to snatch her back from me at the last moment. What kind of mess is that? What did I do wrong? I have walked the straight and narrow with this relationship. You say, "No sex." "Build the friendship, You say." I did that and now that she is my best friend, You take her away. You really need to tell me what's going on. Tell me what to do?" Marcus stops talking in an effort to hear the Lord respond to the tantrum he just threw. All he could hear was dead silence. He finishes drying off and starts to get dressed and realizes its Sunday, the day after what should have been his marriage, the first day of what should have been his honeymoon; and normally he would have been going to church, but today, he has nowhere to go. So instead of getting dressed, he jumps back in bed and falls immediately back to sleep.

Now asleep, Marcus begins to dream. He dreams that he and Zephora are out in the city one day and they are having a great time shopping and visiting friends. Marcus starts out talking to his friends and then he looks up and there is a large crowd of people listening to him speak. There were young people and old people, and the crowd was filled with people from all nationalities. They all stood quietly and listened to Marcus speak. He spoke of change and hope for the future, and of bridging the gap that existed between them. He ended his speech by saying "Change your attitude, change your world," and everyone clapped and cheered him on. He looked to his right at Zephora and knew he could do anything with her by his side. Then out of nowhere, he saw a tornado coming over the horizon, heading right for the crowd of people. Marcus stretched out his arms and a pair of giant bronze wings grew from his back and encircled the crowd of people. The people were screaming with fear as the storm approached, however, surprisingly, Marcus was not afraid and he was able to transfer his quiet confidence to them and through them. Once the storm was directly over them, Marcus looked up into the raging tornado and saw, in the middle of the swirling winds, angels playing golden harps beneath calm clear blue skies. The people in the crowd all kept their heads down under Marcus' wings and never saw the calmness that Marcus was experiencing. Only Zephora lifted her head to see the angels and to experience the peace that Marcus was feeling. Then out of nowhere they heard a voice that proclaimed "Peace be still," and instantly, the storm was gone. Not one person was injured. Marcus removed his wings from around the people, Zephora jumps in his arms, and they fly away with the people cheering them on. They fly over valleys and mountains and then over the ocean gliding peacefully under a rainbow that seemed to stretch out over the entire earth. Just then the phone rings, and Marcus wakes up.

"Hello."

"Baby, you asleep?"

"No Ze, I'm just lying here, trying to rest. How are you doing sweetheart?"

"Marcus, I had a dream that woke me up and the overwhelming thought on my mind was to call you."

"What did you dream about sweetheart?"

"I dreamt we were on an island and we were being chased by men with painted faces and spears. We had to run through the jungle and every time we tried to turn either left or right, different jungle animals would try to attack us. We turned left and there was a lion. If we turned right there would be a rhino. So we kept running straight until we came upon a village that offered to help us. They were very receptive of us and began to adorn you with crowns, jewels, and a royal rope and they even gave you a throne to sit on. When the men that were chasing us caught up to us, they were met and captured by the tribesmen and thrown in a pit. Then all of a sudden, I grew wings, picked you up, and we flew away over the mountains, towards the ocean and under the largest rainbow I have ever seen."

Marcus' eyes are as big as marbles as he listens to Zephora's fantastic dream and notices the similarities to his own. Marcus doesn't think it is time to tell her about his dream, because it would overshadow her moment. "That is an amazing dream. It is filled with hope."

"I could use a little hope right now."

"Well my darling let me tell you something. Hope is only lost when you believe it is. As long as you believe there is hope, hope will always exist."

"Marcus, you always know just what to say to make me feel better. I love you so much."

"I love you so much back."

Marcus is still in shock that they both had dreams of flying away together. Was their subconscious projecting what their hearts wanted to happen, or was it a sign or an answer to the questions he had asked God earlier? Is there really a way out of this madness? What he told Zephora about hope was absolutely right, and after hearing about her dream and comparing it to his own; he had far more hope than he did before she called.

"Ze, I'll come pick you up in an hour, and we'll go have some breakfast and then pick your mother up from the hospital."

"Okay baby, I'll be waiting."

"Say that again, girl."

"Marcus, you are so silly."

"That may be so, but say it again anyway."

"I'll be waiting baby."

"Ooh girl, you turn me on. I'll see you in a minute!"

"I'll be waiting, silly man."

"Don't start none, won't be none."

"Bye baby."

Marcus gets up out of bed, turns the music up, which is always on, and steps into his closet to figure out what to wear. Marcus loves to dress. Sometimes he will go through three or four outfits before he finds the one he wants to wear. It is his first day out in the New Year so he has got to be clean. He pulls out a paprika shirt, brown pants and vest combo, a pair of brown ostrich skin shoes with the matching belt, and then to top it off, a brown brim hat.

Just as Marcus heads towards the door to leave, he hears a light knock on the door, and when he opens the door she falls in and he catches her in his arms. Immediately she snuggles herself in his arms and begins to whimper.

"Oh Marcus, are you alright, I've been so worried about you?"

"Alisha, what are you doing here!?"

"I came to see if you were alright. That was a terrible ordeal, you must be devastated. So I came to take care of you in your time of distress."

"First, get off me, please. Second, I'm not distressed or devastated. And third, how dare you just show up over here, a phone call would have sufficed."

"I knew you needed me baby, so I just decided to come over and cheer you up. See, look!" Alisha steps back and opened her coat to reveal a two piece red matching silk laced bra and panty set that displayed her flawless 5'3", 120 pound, dark chocolate frame with style and perfection, and caused Marcus' bottom lip to drop.

"See now Alisha, this ain't even right. Why do you put yourself out like this? You are far too beautiful and too smart to play yourself like this. Then, when you don't get the response you were looking for, your self-esteem is crushed. Listen, you got to know your self-worth. You're worth more than this Alisha, but if you don't treat yourself like you're worth more, no one else will. I appreciate you coming to check on me, but you should have called, and if we are to remain friends, don't ever try anything like this again. Try respecting yourself as much as I respect you already."

Alisha drops her head and closes her coat. She knows Marcus is right. She has always respected him for never ever taking advantage of her, and always making her think about who she is to herself. "I'm sorry Marcus. I just thought that things would be over between you and Zephora, and I could make you feel better."

"A call from a friend will always make me feel better. I'm actually on my way to pick up Zephora now. Call me later and we can talk more about who you are to you."

"Thanks Marcus. I'll call you, and by the way, you look good enough to eat."

Marcus knows he won't hear from her later because she isn't ready to confront her issues. "Thanks Alisha. Now hold your head up cause you look picture perfect from head to toe."

Alisha gets back in her BMW and drives off disappointed, but is still able to smile because of Marcus' encouraging words. Marcus jumps in his SUV sweating knowing that he just dodged one. "Lord, why are you testing me like that? That heifer looks much too good to be coming to my house like that. I'm glad I was leaving. Damn, she makes it hard on a brother who ain't had none in over a year, and no possibility of getting none anytime soon. I need to shake that off before I pick up Ze. Wait 'til I tell Angelo about this mess. He is not gonna even believe this."

CHAPTER XIII

When Marcus arrives to pick up Zephora, she is ready and impatiently waiting. She always complains that Marcus is always late. Maybe it's all that changing he does in preparation for going out. She has told him before to lay his clothes out the night before, however, even that wouldn't stop Marcus from changing his mind the day of. Whatever the case, again he is late and she is not at all surprised. After all, this is her future husband, or so she still believes, and you have to take the good right along with the bad, and with this man, the pros definitely outweigh the cons.

Marcus greets Zephora at the door like he hadn't seen her in years. He gently pulls her close to him softly pressing his lips against hers, just enough to feel the softness of her moist full lips. Then he wraps his arms around her and hugs her so passionately that she seems to melt in his arms. She is so caught up in his passion and closes her eyes to become totally immersed in his caress. She takes a deep breath and rests her head on his shoulder to get a big sniff of his cologne. As she does, she smells a sweet perfume mixing with it. Zephora is careful not to let the scent ruin this moment; however, she catalogs it to ask him about it later.

"Good morning Marcus baby. Did you miss me?"

"With all my heart and good morning would have been you rolling over in my bed saying that."

"You're absolutely right. My bad; how about I just say morning baby instead?"

"That will do for now until I rectify this situation. Come on let's go. I can't wait to talk to your mother, but how about we go and have breakfast first so I can enjoy being in the presence of such incredible beauty?"

"Thank you baby, but we need to do more than just enjoy each other. We gotta lot of stuff to talk about."

"Not today baby, we will tackle all that stuff tomorrow. Today I just want to be with you, take your mother home, and be with you some more."

"Okay Marcus, but that is so unrealistic."

Marcus walks her to the car and opens the door for her. He places his hand on her butt to help her in. Zephora looks back at him and he just shrugs his shoulders and smiles. She watches him walk around the front of the car and still has that perfume she smelled on her mind. Zephora is a smart girl, and she patiently awaits the opportunity to confront him. Marcus makes his way around the SUV, gets in, buckles up, looks over at Zephora, smiles and notices the smirk on her face and pulls off.

"Oh, by the way, you'll never guess what happened to me this morning." Marcus is a smart dude. He realized that Zephora could smell Alisha's perfume and decided that the best defense is a good offense.

"Do tell baby." Zephora responds with a hint of irritation in her voice.

"As I was about to leave my house, Alisha showed up at my door."

"Oh really now. Whatever did she want?"

"She said she came by to check on me and see if there was anything she could do to help me feel better about what happened."

"I bet she did. Obviously, she had her hands all over you. Not that I blame her because you look so scrumptious baby."

"Thank you baby. Yeah, she thought she would come over and cheer me up, and she really came prepared to do just that. I told her a phone call would have been good enough, and not to show up at my house like that again."

"And how did you get her perfume all over you?"

"Well, as I was opening the door she was knocking and she just sort of fell through and I caught her. She faked a cry and tried to hold on to me as long as possible before I pushed her away and told her to have some self-respect."

"I don't want you to talk to her anymore, she's bad news."

"Ze, I don't want to argue about this, but I will say this; you don't have to worry about her or any other woman. It's not about them anyway, it's about me. My devotion is to you, my loyalty is to you, and hopefully, I have proven myself trustworthy to you. Furthermore, I love you with every fiber of my being, and I would not let any woman destroy what we share. I can't control other people's actions, just my own. And if I disowned every person that made a mistake, and in my book, the first time is a mistake, I couldn't associate with anyone, not even myself."

"Okay Marcus, you made your point, but if that heifer tries that mess again, I'm beating her down."

"As long as I can watch; now, let's talk about you and how extraordinarily beautiful you look today with your fine self." Marcus had successfully defended his honor and circumvented any future incidents that should occur with any other nut that may try him.

"Thank you baby. I gotta look good to be on your arm."

And with that said they both glance at each other and smile. Together they are a formidable pair. They complement one another so well. Marcus decides to take Zephora to I-Hop for breakfast. They arrive at the restaurant and there is a twenty minute wait. They take a seat out front holding hands watching the other patrons and making jokes about them. Finally they are seated, and enjoy a great meal and great conversation on everything except their current dilemma.

It's hard to beat having a mate you enjoy spending all your time with, and that is just the kind of relationship that Marcus and Zephora share. The crisis they are in now has done nothing but bring them closer together. In the face of such drama, they are still able to laugh and have a good time.

Mostly due to Marcus, he refuses to worry or let anything get him down. He is noted for saying that his faith allows him not to worry, and to just do his part and let God do His.

Now on their way to pick up Saphera, the dialogue turns serious. It centers around confronting Saphera on the part she has played in hiding the truth about Zephora's heritage. Despite Marcus' efforts, their nice morning is now filled with the anxiety of the looming contract and what to do about it. Marcus assures Zephora that he would be doing everything within his power to correct this injustice. They had taken weeks off work and away from business for their honeymoon, however, since they won't be going right now, Marcus plans to use the time to get with his attorney to resolve this minor setback as quickly as possible.

Marcus and Zephora walk through the front door of the hospital and the place is buzzing. Doctors and nurses are running around as though there is an emergency on every floor. As the two ease down the hall to Saphera's room, they notice that all the commotion seemed to be coming in and out of her room.

"Oh my God Marcus, what's going on? I just talked to her a few hours ago and she was looking forward to coming home."

"I don't know baby, but I'll go and find out." Marcus pulls one of the doctors down the hall aside and questions him.

"Mss. Sherman has taken a turn for the worse and we can't isolate the problem. She is running a high fever and she is having trouble breathing and has been having occasional seizures. She was fine an hour ago, and then her vital signs started to dip. We are doing all we can. The important thing is to run some more blood tests to find out exactly what is going on. We are quarantining the room until we figure this thing out, so I can't allow you to go in there."

"Okay, but let us know as soon as you find out."

Marcus grabs Zephora and takes her down the hall to the all but to familiar waiting area and explains the situation to her. With all the pressure she is feeling, she immediately breaks down and starts to cry. All Marcus can do is hold her until she gets it all out. He knows exactly how she is feeling and there are no words to be said at this moment, just comforting her has to be enough, and he has shoulders strong enough to do just that.

There is a knock on Kwazan's hotel room door and one of his guard's proceeds to open it.

"Sir, its LaNok."

"Let him in. Report LaNok."

"Your instructions have been followed to the letter. Everything is in order. Here is the solution to the problem," LaNok states as he hands a package over. "You have five days, and after that, it will be too late."

"Are you sure it will work?"

"Absolutely, you pay me to be sure."

"Good. Follow my associate here to the back and he will pay you."

"Thank you sir."

LaNok follows the guard to the back room of the suite where they are met by Kwazan's other bodyguard. The first guard breaks LaNok's neck; they then wrap him in plastic and then a large rug. They smile at one another like they had been waiting to do something like this for a long time.

"It's done sir. We'll dispose of the body shortly."

"Just make sure you are not seen by anyone."

CHAPTER XIV

It's Monday morning, and Marcus and Zephora have been at the hospital all night. Marcus finally got Zephora to calm down and as soon as he did, she went straight to sleep and stayed that way all night with her head in his lap. His leg had fallen asleep hours ago, yet he refused to get up for fear of disturbing Zephora's sleep. Marcus is extremely concerned that the doctors have not come out to talk to them and that they have no idea what caused Saphera's drastic turn around. One minute she was fine, the next she wasn't. It was like something out of a movie. Marcus, who is naturally suspicious, allows his mind to wonder about the different things that could have happened as he watches his baby rest.

Mr. Netumba receives a report from his men who are watching Kwazan. They report seeing Kwazan's men carrying something large out of the hotel and put it in the trunk of their car. They ask him if they should follow them. He tells them to do just that. They proceed to follow them staying at least four cars back. His other team who is keeping tabs on Marcus and Zephora, report Saphera's sudden declining health.

Mr. Netumba instinctively understands the seriousness of the situation, he has seen it before. He knows what will come next and decides he must move his plans ahead faster than anticipated.

It's 1:00 p.m., and Charlie receives a call in her hotel room. It's Mr. Netumba and he is coming to take her to lunch. He sounded flustered so Charlie was more anxious than excited. When he arrives, Charlie leaves her grandmother and father to fend for themselves as she goes to meet with her new friend. Over lunch, Mr. Netumba informs Charlie that they must move their time table up. Instead of leaving for the Bahamas in two weeks, they need to leave in a couple of days. Charlie agrees and decides to stay in Atlanta with her brother and let Jackson and Ruth go back to Florida without her. Mr. Netumba tells her he will buy her all new clothes for the trip.

Now back from lunch, Charlie proceeds to inform her grandmother of her intentions. Ruth, being the wise woman that she is, gives Charlie her blessings and tells her to be careful and to make sure she gets the truth. Charlie tries to act like she has no idea what her grandmother is talking about. Ruth, with her quick tongue responds "I was born at night, but it wasn't last night." They both laugh and Charlie gives her a big hug. Charlie's next mission is to inform Jackson of her change of plans. Jackson, much like Ruth, is not surprised by Charlie's choice. In fact, he was waiting on her when she knocked on the door. Jackson is not known for his tact, so when she comes in, he attempts to give it to her with both barrels.

"Now Charlie, I know you're a grown woman and you don't need my approval…."

"I most assuredly don't."

"Listen, what I'm trying to say is this; take these papers with you. Find this company and its owner and you'll find the rest of what you've been looking for. I'm very proud of you for doing this."

"Doing what?" Charlie is trying her best to figure out how everyone knows more about what she is doing than she does.

"Listen girl. We don't see eye to eye on a lot of things, and I know I haven't been a good father, but I do love you very much."

"Thanks daddy and I appreciate your help."

"Now who is this guy you are going with?"

"Don't worry about it; he's none of your business. After that great speech you just made, don't ruin it by prying."

Jackson knows from experience to quit while he's ahead. He agrees reluctantly to make sure Ruth gets back home safely, and Charlie agrees to be careful.

It's 6:00 p.m., and Saphera has been moved to ICU. Her condition is still critical, but stable. The doctors have concluded that she has somehow contracted a deadly virus. They are still analyzing the data from her blood tests to determine what particular virus she has. After getting the news, Marcus has finally convinced Zephora that they should leave and come back in the morning. They decided that Zephora should spend the night at Marcus' home. Just as they are leaving the hospital, Marcus gets a phone call and even though he doesn't recognize the number, he decides to answer it anyway.

"Hello."

"Marcus, this is Kwazan. Have you had time to check out the contract with your attorney today?"

"No Kwazan I haven't. We have been at the hospital all day with Saphera. Her condition has taken a change for the worse."

"I am sorry to hear that. How is Zephora and is there anything that I can do?"

"She is fine, and we have everything we need thank you."

"I will come by the hospital in the morning."

"That's not necessary Kwazan."

"I insist. She is my future mother-in-law and I want to make sure she is going to be alright. Plus, I would love to speak with Zephora again."

"That is yet to be determined. Anyway, call me in the morning and we'll see what happens."

Marcus hangs up and takes Zephora to her home to get clothes and personal items before they continue on to his home. Marcus is a gentleman in every sense of the word. Though Zephora is staying with him, he refuses to allow her to sleep with him or even bunk with him. His home has two extra guest bedrooms. Marcus willingly gives Zephora his master suite because it is more comfortable and he takes the guest room down the hall. Marcus cooks dinner for his distraught fiancé; they watch a little television and then settle in for the night. He can only imagine that this is how it would have been if they had successfully gotten married. The thought of it causes him great anguish and he ends up lying in bed staring at the ceiling.

Kwazan is feeling quite content with himself. His plans are working perfectly. Tomorrow, he plans to put the finishing touches on them and claim his prize.

CHAPTER XV

Marcus let Zephora sleep in, she had a rough night. She tossed and turned all night. She seemed to be having nightmares all night. They were so intense that Marcus decided to sleep in the recliner in the room with her to watch over her, plus he wasn't getting any sleep anyway running back and forth from room to room either. At least from the chair he didn't have to go so far. He didn't know that Zephora talked in her sleep, or in this case, yelled and snarled in her sleep. She only started resting peacefully around 4:00 a.m., so he decided to let her sleep until at least ten. Marcus is an early riser, and no matter what happens or how bad he slept, he is still usually awake by 5:00 a.m. However, this morning he chose to give himself a break and slept in his chair until eight, after which, he got up and went through his normal morning routine.

With Zephora still sleep, Marcus went downstairs put on some coffee and read his Bible. He always finds comfort when he reads the Word. He knows that the answers to life's questions are all there. He just hopes he can find the answer he is looking for now. During his reading, he heard the voice of the Lord speaking to him. Marcus had chosen long ago to build a personal relationship with God, and because he maintains and nurtures this relationship, he is able to discern the still quiet voice of God. He may not always listen, but he does know His voice. This morning God said *"Be slow to anger."* Slow to anger about what, Marcus thought. Is Zephora going to wake up in a foul mood and start a fight? I can handle that. Even though Marcus didn't understand it, he let the words resonate in his spirit. He prayed for the wisdom to discern the meaning of God's message to him. He also prayed for Saphera's speedy recovery.

It's 10:00 a.m. and Zephora is finally awake. She notices that Marcus isn't there and then smells the coffee he has brewing downstairs. She rolls out of bed, brushes her teeth, washes her face, takes a shower and gets dressed. As she reaches the bottom of the stairs, Marcus is standing there waiting for her. He greets her with a long embrace, followed by a deep passionate kiss that arouses Zephora from the rooter to the tooter. She responded by stroking his bald head with one hand, pulling him closer with the other, and kissing him with more passion and zeal than he had previously exhibited. This stimulates him to the core, and she could immediately feel it.

"Good morning my love."

"Good morning Marcus. Man, I had a nightmare that we didn't get married and my mother was in the hospital in critical condition, but with a good morning kiss like that, I know it must have all been a dream."

"Unfortunately it's not. And that nightmare you're referring to is actually our reality."

"That's too bad baby, because I was about to tell you to take me upstairs, shower me with kisses, and make sweet gentle love to me like only a husband can."

"Oh well, I hope you will settle for breakfast instead."

Marcus knows better than to continue to indulge in Zephora's fantasy. He has wanted to give her his love on a physical plane for a long time, and if he allows himself the luxury of indulgence, he knows he will not be strong enough to resist giving her exactly what she is asking for, and a whole lot more. He gets aroused just by thinking about her smile, so having his hands wrapped around her beautiful firm but soft body, kissing her soft lips, and holding her so close to himself, alone in his home, is almost certainly more than he can handle. He has often fantasized about the way he will make love to her for the first time. How she will feel in his arms, how the warmth of her naked body next to his will take him higher than any drug, and how he will slowly and methodically make love to every inch of her mind and body, by caressing the crown of her head to sucking on her littlest toe. But today's reality is breakfast, best to focus only on that.

Marcus prepared a delicious and nutritious breakfast of organic eggs scrambled with spinach, mushrooms, cheese and tomatoes, turkey sausage, whole wheat pancakes, and a bowl of fruit topped off with coffee and freshly squeezed orange juice.

"Is this what I can expect every day when we're married?"

"Not every day, but sometimes."

"Good, because if I eat like this every day, I'll be as big as a house."

"Nope, 'cause after breakfast we would go upstairs and workout for a while."

"So is it time for our workout?"

"Don't tempt me girl, 'cause I will take you upstairs and change your life."

"Down boy, your day is coming. And when it gets here, that is just what you'll be doing, so keep saving it up. But for now, sit back and relax while I clean this kitchen."

Marcus leans back in his chair and watches Zephora wash the dishes. Her jeans perfectly accentuate her round butt, and end at her flat stomach and neat waist. His eyes continue to move up her body to her perky 36C cups, to her smooth and slender neck, her shoulder length black shiny hair, big beautiful light brown eyes, and stops at her full lips adorned with a soft red lipstick. Instantly, he gets pissed because all this is supposed to be his to enjoy right now. *"Be slow to anger,"* rings in his head and he laughs to himself.

Breakfast done, dishes washed, and out the door, and they made it without ripping each other's clothes off. As they are riding, Marcus reaches over to hold Zephora's hand. She clinches his tight and he raises her hand and softly kisses the back of it. That was the first night they had ever spent together alone under the same roof. Even when they travel together, they would get separate rooms. Their physical attraction for one another is just as strong as the rest of the love they share. Marcus is not looking forward to tempting himself another night; she is going to have to stay at her house tonight, or he won't be responsible for his actions.

When they enter the hospital doors, the first person they see is Kwazan, who stands six feet three inches tall and is a well-built handsome dark skin toned brother with a strong chiseled chin; and behind him, are his gruesome twosome both standing around six feet five inches and buffed. Marcus starts to recite his Word for the day, "be slow to anger, be slow to anger, be slow to anger," and now he understands their purpose. He had asked Kwazan to call him before coming down here, but obviously, Kwazan doesn't follow instructions very well.

"Good morning you two, how glad I am to see you."

"Well, it was a good morning until we saw you."

"Marcus my friend, the feeling is mutual. I was just trying to be cordial."

The hospital's automatic doors open up again. Marcus turns and looks back and is pleasantly surprised to see his good buddy Angelo walking through them; however, the light from the outside was so bright that it wasn't until he got all the way in that Marcus was able to recognize him.

"Angelo, what are you doing here my brotha?"

"Zephora texted Veronica last night, she in turn texted me and here I am, and apparently, right on time."

"Nothing I can't handle, but I'm glad to see you anyway."

The two of them hug Angelo, Angelo and Zephora hug, and they all act as if Kwazan is not even standing there. This of course, annoyed Kwazan. He thinks he should be the center of attention.

"Excuse me gentlemen, I hate to break up your reunion, but it is imperative that I speak with Zephora."

Zephora quickly responds, "Whatever you have to say to me, you can say to my fiancé too."

"He was your fiancé, I am now. But have it your way. I took the liberty of reserving this little conference room, so if you will both follow me, we can begin."

Marcus and Zephora follow Kwazan into the conference room. His guards and Angelo stay outside in the main waiting area. Once in the room, Marcus takes a seat directly in front of Kwazan and Zephora sits to Marcus' right. They both stare at him intensely in anticipation of what he has to say.

"What I have to say may be very upsetting. Please try to control whatever emotions you might have, because my guards will enter at the drop of a hat."

Zephora grabs Marcus' hand and is noticeably worried.

"Just get to it Kwazan."

"Okay then, I poisoned your mother Zephora, with a deadly African virus."

Marcus jumps to his feet and shouts, "You low-life son of a b....!" he bites down on his bottom lip to keep from cursing and rushes toward Kwazan.

"Not so fast Marcus, one word from me and my guards will enter; besides, there is more. I have the only antivirus serum that you can get in time to save her life. If not administered within two and a half days, she will die. I will not give her the serum until you two agree to sign this letter that states you agree to the terms of the Tribal Law Contract, to Zephora marrying me and taking her place by my side on the throne of my people. Furthermore, I forbid you to see Marcus anymore after today. However, the choice is yours. I will leave the room while you think it over. But remember, you have very little time to waste."

Marcus and Zephora are stunned. Zephora immediately begins to cry and Marcus grinds his teeth. Being slow to anger has reached its peak and Marcus is ready to rip Kwazan's head off. Why would he do this unless the contract is void? Doesn't matter now, a life hangs in the balance and their choice will decide Saphera's fate.

PART 4

SACRIFICE, COMMITMENT & DEATH

CHAPTER XVI

When they woke up this morning, there is no way Marcus or Zephora could have predicted what just happened. Who would have thought that Kwazan was not just a wedding crasher, but a murderer too? If he is willing to go to these lengths to get Zephora, there is no telling what else he is capable of doing or has already done to get his way. Though furious, Marcus knows he must keep his cool because not only is Saphera's life in danger, but probably his own. In his mind, the decision is an easy one to make, it's what to do afterwards that counts.

Zephora is in shock. Not only is this man threatening her mother's life, but he actually expects her to marry him. How could she possibly go through with something like that? The first thing on her mind is saving her mother. Once this has been accomplished, she figures she can decide what to do next. She thinks about calling the police for help, but that might trigger Kwazan and jeopardize her mother's life. One thing she knows for sure is that she trusts Marcus and knows he will come up with a plan. She has no problem putting her life in his hands.

"Okay Ze, this is an easy choice to make. We must first save Saphera, and then we can work on nailing this guy. However, unless I miss my guess, he probably has diplomatic immunity. There is nothing we can do here, it must be done in Africa, and we must be able to prove it."

"Marcus, how can you be so calm at a time like this? All this is making me crazy."

"I don't know, but while I was reading the Bible this morning, the Lord spoke to me and said to be slow to anger. So I have made a conscious effort to do that and it is helping me stay calm. Not to mention, when I am calm, my heart and mind are clear to hear God speak, and He will tell me what to do and say next."

"This cannot be happening. You are everything I need in a man. How can I lose you, especially since I know with everything in me that you are the half that makes me whole?"

"Ditto baby, and right now I'm going to do everything in my power to make sure that you don't."

"Okay Marcus, I'm listening, tell me what to do."

Marcus knows he needs concrete evidence against Kwazan in order to make it stick, and because Kwazan is a dignitary from another country, there is nothing the US government will do to help. He must make this happen himself. He explains his plan to Zephora and she agrees that it is a good one, and the only way to rid them of this menace. After working out all the details, they call Kwazan back into the room and begin to execute their plan.

"Okay Kwazan, you win, you're holding all the cards. But tell me, how were you able to pull this off and why?"

"Well Marcus, I was raised to do whatever it takes to get what I want. Anyone and anything in my way can be easily removed just by aligning myself with the right people. And my family has been watching Zephora for a long time. Her mother has done an excellent job of raising her and preparing her to be queen."

"You mean she knew they were being watched and worked with you?"

"Not really. Saphera was instructed by her husband, Zephora's father, to raise her in a regal manner. The contract I have is very real. It was signed by both my father and Zephora's father; however, the circumstances by which he signed it had been left out. My father was the one who trained me in this delicate art of negotiation, and the one who had Zephora's father killed."

"You bastard! You killed my father and robbed me of having him around just so you could have me? Did it ever occur to you people to get to know me and I might have chosen you instinctively?"

"You must understand, the wheels were put in motion a long, long time ago. I did not have the luxury of getting to know you."

"So now to finish what your father started, you are here threatening my mother's life too?"

"Your mother is just a pawn in all of this. Even though she has a strong African heritage, she is just a means to an end."

"Why is it so important that you have me? Surely your people don't follow all the old laws. They can't possibly be as important as they once were. You could marry anyone and say they are the heir. My whole family is dead, who would ever know?"

"You are wrong about that. For centuries these laws have been honored and I am not about to break the cycle. Sure, there are outside forces that affect us now that had not been present before, but our sacred Tribal Laws have always prevailed. Our two tribes control most of the leaders of many African countries and have done so for centuries. And as for marrying anyone, it is not possible. The DNA of all the original noble families is locked away and guarded. So anyone I bring would be tested. You were tested years ago, that is why I know for sure that you are the one."

"Why have we never heard about any of this?"

"Do you know about all of the secret societies that control this country? Do you know the power that the Masons and the Shriners possess, or that the Roman Catholic Church controls most of the leaders of the free world? No, you do not because these are all well kept secrets and people have died and will continue to die to keep them. The same can be said about our respective tribes' influence in Africa. Now, enough with the history lesson sign these papers and save your Mother's life."

"Not until you tell us how you did it. How did you poison Saphera?"

"I hired someone, who consequently will never speak of his deed, to put the virus in her I.V. The only reason I am telling you this is because you, Marcus, you are a nobody, and cannot prove it, and you, Zephora, are going to be my queen and after we are married and you bare my child, I can arrange the same for you if you do not cooperate. Now sign the papers!"

"Not until you give Saphera the antidote and her condition improves."

"I am giving you my word and that should be enough."

"The word of a murderer means nothing to a nobody like me."

"I have not lied to you, and I have only done what I had to do to protect my people."

"Just the same, I don't trust you. So first the antidote, and then the contract will be signed."

"Fine, stay here, I will be back shortly."

"Send my friend Angelo in on your way out."

"Sure, but tell him anything and I will have him killed, and you too, Marcus."

"You've made your point Kwazan. Now go do your part."

Marcus and Zephora have learned far more than they had expected. Kwazan was more than willing to tell all he knew because he doesn't view Marcus as a threat. However, all his revealing information has played right into Marcus' hand, and little does Kwazan know that the information he so willingly provided will eventually come back to haunt him. Marcus looks at Zephora and smiles, but inside himself he knows that his life is in danger now. He must take every precaution, and be aware of everything around him if he is going to live long enough to carry out his plan. Marcus feels it is all worth the risk, because he knows that Zephora is worth it. She may not marry him, but he plans to make for certain that she doesn't marry Kwazan either.

As Kwazan leaves the conference room, he sends Angelo in and sends one of his aids, who is dressed like a doctor, to Saphera's room to administer the antidote. It will be a few hours before it will take effect, and gives Kwazan some time to kill. He is by no means a stupid individual. He has gotten this far by effectively covering his tracks. And now that he has told all his dirty little secrets to Marcus and Zephora, he must do damage control. He has decided that after the papers are signed, he will have no further use for Marcus. Marcus knows too much, and it would be better to eliminate the problem than have it lingering out there. He tells his guards to make it look like an accident. They are more than happy to carry out his orders. Kwazan is very arrogant and full of himself; killing has become so easy to him now, and he feels it is an effective way to solve his problems. Kwazan thinks to himself, "My father would be so proud."

CHAPTER XVII

Angelo walks into the conference room, and by looking at Marcus and Zephora, he can't tell what is going on. All he knows is that regardless of the circumstances, he is ready for battle. With Angelo, it seems he is always ready for battle, looking to pounce on anyone or anything at the drop of a hat. In the past, when he and Marcus were out together, Marcus spent a lot of time keeping him calm. He's like a wind up doll, pull the string and watch him go. Angelo has been known to take out two or three guys at one time by himself, and beat them all. He has a black belt in karate and isn't afraid to use it. He and Marcus sometimes spar together to keep their abilities and agility sharp. However, unfortunately for Angelo, the mission Marcus has for him doesn't include breaking anyone's head.

"Angelo my friend, it seems that you are always in the right place at the right time. Come in and have a seat, we have much to talk about and not a lot of time to do it in."

"Okay, whose head needs smashing this time?"

"Boy you will never change, but I like it. However this time I have something else for you my friend. That is if you would be so kind as to accept it."

"Accept what Marcus? What are you talking about?"

"I want you as the Executive Vice President of my company. We have talked about it from time to time, and I feel now is the time to make it happen. Business is good, you're an excellent businessman and I trust you with my life. So, how about it?"

"This is kind of sudden Marcus, what's really going on?"

"I can't go into all the details right now, but I have to go out of the country for a minute to try and pick up some new clients, and I need someone here that I trust to run things."

"Marcus, you know I'm down with you for whatever. You paying me or am I doing this on the strength?"

"Of course I'm paying. This is not a temporary situation, this is permanent. Look at the number on this paper and tell me if it's enough or not."

Marcus slides a piece of paper across to Angelo. Business has been great for some time now and he is willing and able to pay top dollar to Angelo for his services. He knows the amount is nearly twice as much as Angelo is making. This really won't matter to Angelo, he'll just be happy to finally be working with his best friend just like they dreamed. When Angelo looks at the paper, his eyes get big with excitement, but he tries to play it off.

"Is that all? Let me think about it." Angelo pauses for a minute. Marcus and Zephora look at each other, and then Angelo blurts out, "Heck yeah it's enough! When do I start?"

"Monday, if that's not too soon because that will give us a chance to get you familiar with our procedures and our people."

"Monday, what do I tell my current employer?"

"I need you man. Just quit. I'll give you a starting bonus."

"No need for that brother, I didn't like the job anyway, or my boss."

"Thank you. I'm glad to have you on board, finally. It seems we have been trying to make this happen for years."

"Yeah, thanks man. I can't wait to tell Veronica."

"Who? What?"

"You heard me right. I really dig her man."

"Bro, that's great. I knew…."

"Excuse me," Zephora interrupts. "We do have business to tend to boys."

"You're right baby. Let me get back to it. Angelo, can you beam a recorded conversation to your phone from my phone?"

"I don't think that's possible."

"Can you download a recorded conversation from your phone to the computer or to a disk?"

"I believe so, provided that the phone's information disk has been downloaded on your computer."

"Good, because since we all have the same type of phone, I need you to take Zephora's and download the recorded info and put it on three disks. Do this discreetly and don't listen to it unless you get a call from Ze. That's very important. We'll leave here later on and I want you to drop one off to Ze, put one in your safety deposit box, and bring one to me at my house."

"Sure man, but what's up? Why all the cloak and dagger stuff?"

"I can't explain it now, but I promise I will later. Can you go and take care of this now?"

"Is this my first official duty? Just kidding, I got you covered man. I'll see ya later."

Zephora and Angelo switch phones and then he heads out to accomplish his mission. Marcus and Zephora both recorded the conversation with Kwazan on their phones. Getting it on disk is just insurance, better to be prepared and not need it, than to need it and not be prepared. Part one of Marcus' plan is complete; however, he feels his life will be in danger as soon as those papers are signed. He begins to formulate a plan to keep his head above ground long enough to get Kwazan behind bars.

The men who Mr. Netumba have watching Kwazan's guards took pictures of the two dumping a body at a nearby landfill; they report this news back to Mr. Netumba and proceed to follow them back to the hotel and then to the hospital. So far they have gone undetected. They have been instructed to keep their distance, but not too loose site of

Kwazan and his crew. The team he has watching Marcus and Zephora have reported the meeting that the two had with Kwazan. Mr. Netumba knows that Kwazan has made his move and now Marcus' life is probably in danger. He tells his men to stay with Marcus at all costs, and to do whatever it takes to keep him safe. He doesn't have to worry about Zephora right now; Kwazan won't hurt her because she is his prize.

Mr. Netumba's men are well trained, ex-special forces members. They do excellent stealth work, seek and destroy work, and will take a life or give their own to accomplish their objectives. Mr. Netumba, though a lot older is a highly trained operative too, one of the government's best. With all of his men in place, he now has time to focus on his plans with Charlie; they are equally as important to him.

The doctor is both confused and excited as he comes to get Marcus and Zephora. He shares with them that miraculously Saphera's condition has changed for the better, and her vital signs have returned to normal. "Whatever made her sick, has run its course and her body has fought off the virus." Zephora is overjoyed and leaps into Marcus' arms and holds him tightly as tears fall from her eyes. The doctor informs them that she will be moved to a private room and as long as her condition continues to improve, she can probably go home at the end of the week.

Kwazan has kept his word. Now, the papers must be signed. Marcus is seriously dreading this part of the deal. He must agree not to see Zephora anymore, not to call her or communicate with her in any way after tonight. Since they started dating, there hasn't been a day that they haven't communicated with each other in some way. This will be extremely hard on Zephora and he is worried if she will be able to handle it. After all, he is leaving her in the hands of a mad man. They head back to the conference room to strategize their situation. Kwazan has no problem giving them all the time they need there. Kwazan knows this is the last day they will see one another. He has won the day and the prize he has gone to great lengths to acquire.

The stress of the state of affairs has begun to weigh heavily on Zephora. She tries to come to grips with the possibility of this being the last day she will ever see Marcus, and the tears begin to stream down her face. Marcus, on the other hand, has not conceded and is still in planning mode. He stops and takes the time to comfort Zephora, and then directs his attentions towards getting their plans organized.

"Okay Ze, listen, we have to get on the same page."

"I'm trying baby, but I'm worried I might not ever see you again."

"One of the things that I have grown to love about you is your ability to work through problems. This one is no different. Remember your dream baby, and don't worry. We got this guy dead to rights. Signing the papers is just a formality, but we must do it on our terms no matter what. So tell him you need sixty days to plan the wedding you have always dreamed of, and do just that, and make sure he agrees that it takes place here."

"Okay Marcus, whatever you say. But what are you going to be doing?'

"I'll be taking a trip to Africa and exposing Kwazan to his fellow council members."

"Marcus this had better work. I don't want to marry this clown. My life is literally in your hands now."

"I know baby, and I don't plan on failing because without you, I have no life. You are my sunshine, my cool breeze on a hot day, the air I breathe and my happily ever after. Now let's pray and ask God for His blessings."

The two stand up, hold hands, bow their heads and Marcus begins to pray. He gives a heartfelt, spirit filled prayer in which he asks for wisdom, courage, strength and favor for them both. Zephora follows him with a prayer for protection and guidance and especially God's grace. The two hug and give praise to God and worship Him. Marcus explains to Zephora that struggle is a part of every person's life; the greater the struggle the greater the reward once through the struggle. His faith is strong and he assures Zephora that as long as they put God first in their lives, and do their part, God is faithful to do His. It's not the struggle, but being able to praise God through the struggle that really matters. She smiles as she stares into his eyes. She would follow him anywhere. No matter what, he is the king of her heart.

CHAPTER XVIII

Kwazan is all smiles as he enters the conference room. He has achieved his objective, and with minimal loss of life. With briefcase in hand, he takes a seat at the end of the table, opens his briefcase, and slides one contract to Marcus and one to Zephora. The one he gives to Marcus is for him to agree not to communicate with Zephora after today. Marcus is amazed that the contract has the correct date and time at the top and laughs about it as he shows it to Zephora. Zephora's contract has her committing to marry this century's one and true heir of the Great Zimbabwean tribe. As this century's one and true heir to the Mapungubwe people, she must marry him within 45 days of signing the contract.

Marcus and Zephora read over the information on each other's contract and agree to the terms with the exception of the 45 day rule. They ask for 60 days instead, for the wedding to take place here, and for Marcus to be able to attend the wedding. Kwazan agrees to the changes and both parties sign off on them. For Kwazan, Marcus being at the wedding is a welcomed bonus because it establishes his authority and superiority over Marcus. Besides, if he has his way, it won't matter because he doesn't expect Marcus to make it to tomorrow.

"Now that your contracts are signed Kwazan, can you leave us alone for a bit?"

"Why sure Marcus, you only have a few more hours with her anyway. I am going back to my hotel. Zephora, I will leave the details of our wedding to you and your mother. My advisors will be available to you day and night. I will pay for everything so make it a day you will remember forever. I expect everything to be ready and on time. I will call you in 30 days to find out where it will be and besides that I will have no other communication with you before we get married. And Marcus, I expect you to keep your word."

"You need not worry about me Kwazan, I, unlike you, am a man of honor. After I take Ze home, I will not see her again as promised until the day of the wedding. Now get out, you're infringing on my time."

"Be careful my friend, you are addressing royalty."

"You may be royalty somewhere, but here, you are just another man. So I suggest you go run to your guards before I put my size twelve foot in your royal butt!"

"The threats of a defeated man mean nothing to me."

And with that, Kwazan laughs and leaves the room. As he and his entourage leave the hospital, he turns to address his guards. He grabs them both by their collars, looks them both in their eyes and proclaims, "After he drops off Zephora and goes home, I want him dead, and do not come back without proof of his death. It is his life or your own lives. Am I understood?"

They reply in one loud harmonic voice, "Yes your highness!"

Marcus and Zephora head down the hall to Saphera's new room. When they get there and go in, they are amazed to see her sitting up and eating. She is unhooked from all the breathing and monitoring machines, and only her I.V. remains.

"Hi you two, why the long faces; I'm doing fine now. I don't know what happened, but I'm feeling much, much better."

"That's great Mother. I can't wait to get you out of here and back home."

"Yeah Mss. Sherman, it is good to see you up and smiling. You gave us all a pretty good scare."

"Okay you two, I wasn't born yesterday, something is wrong. What happened while I was out?"

"A lot mother, a whole lot."

"Well tell me my child and put my head to rest."

"Mss. Sherman please let me explain."

Zephora takes a seat in the corner and Marcus takes the time to explain step by step the events of the last few days. He goes into great detail rehashing everything from her being poisoned by Kwazan, to his death threats and contracts, to the antidote for her recovery. Saphera is so shocked that she drops her fork and stops eating. Suddenly, she begins to cry because she knows this is mostly her fault. She had ignored this situation for years and never even bothered to mention it to her daughter. Had she dealt with this years ago it may not be plaguing their lives now. Saphera is heartbroken and can't apologize enough through her tears for mishandling this important obligation to her daughter.

Zephora, unmoved by her mother's display of snot and tears, shakes her head in disgust and finally agrees to accept her mother's apology. What's done is done, they must now work together to stop this wedding to a mad man from ever happening. Saphera asks for her purse. When Zephora brings it to her, she reaches in a side pocket and pulls out a key.

"This key is to our safety deposit box. Before you come to pick me up and take me home, go to the bank and bring the contents of the box with you. Don't try to read any of it, just bring it to me and we will go through it all together."

"Oh, you mean the safety deposit box I know nothing about? Will do Mother, but when we do go through its contents, be sure not to leave out any details. We're leaving now. Marcus is going to take me home and spend what little time he has left with me since I won't see him for at least 60 days."

"Zephora sweetheart," Saphera begs, "I am so sorry. I never, ever expected anything like this to happen. Marcus, listen to me."

"Yes ma'am," Marcus replies.

"I believe in you, I don't know why, but I do. You go to Africa and find the council and expose Kwazan. You will probably find them in Lilongwe, the capitol of Malawi. My prayers are and will be with you. Be careful and come home safely."

"Thank you Mss. Sherman, that is very helpful, and don't worry about me, just get better, take good care of my

Zephora and I will see you when I get back. I do have one question; why Malawi?"

Saphera informatively responds, "When the two tribes moved north, Malawi is the country they settled in and founded; one tribe in the southern part of the country and the other in the north. What is widely unknown to the outside world is the mountain of wealth the country possesses. The two tribes control access to it. This is why you must be careful."

Marcus and Zephora leave Saphera's room, and the hospital still holding hands. They spoke no words, got in the car, and just continued to hold hands. Marcus' mind is focused on being aware. He can feel he is being watched and mentally he is preparing for what he thinks will be a showdown. Zephora is now in a state of depression. She can't believe all this is happening to her. It's like some crazy movie. Her time with Marcus is running short and she doesn't know what she will do without him.

CHAPTER XIX

Kwazan's guards have dropped him off back at the hotel and are now posted down the street from Zephora's house. Just out of their view is another car. It has two of Mr. Netumba's men in it and they are watching Kwazan's guards for their next move. The chess game is on and Kwazan is at a disadvantage because he doesn't know all the players. Equally so, Marcus doesn't know all the players either; however, unbeknown to him, he has the advantage because the extra unknown players are on his side.

As Marcus rolls down Zephora's street and pulls in her driveway, he notices Kwazan's men, but doesn't let Zephora know anything is going on. Zephora is too preoccupied to notice anything other than Marcus. The two enter the house Marcus locks the front door and does a security check of all the doors and windows. After that he closes all the blinds and curtains. Zephora heads upstairs and Marcus turns on the living room light and takes a seat on the couch which faces the front door. His senses are on high alert. He knows they are being watched and hopes the goons will wait until he leaves before they make their move. He assumes they wouldn't risk Zephora getting hurt. Either way, he makes himself aware of his surroundings for defense of an attack. Like Angelo,

Marcus has a black belt but in Judo; however, that is no defense against guns fired from a distance.

When Zephora comes back downstairs, she has changed into a sexy black two piece negligee. Marcus' bottom lip drops and his eyes grow three sizes. This is the first time he has seen his woman in such a revealing ensemble, and he is not disappointed.

"If this is going to be the last night I'm going to see you, we might as well make the best of it."

"Ze, you might want to stay on that side of the room before something jumps off up in here."

"That's the whole idea Marcus. Relax, don't fight it baby; you know you want what I'm offering."

"Girl, I've wanted you since the first time I laid eyes on you, but....."

"No buts. Here I am and I'm all yours."

Zephora glides over, straddles Marcus on the couch, gently grabs his face and begins to softly kiss his face in every available place ending at his lips which she kisses passionately. Marcus is overcome with pleasure, closes his eyes, accepts her kisses and returns with some of own. His body is ready and willing, his mind and spirit are not. He must get out of there to protect her from harm. He knows she isn't going to like it, but he has no choice. He takes his time, and wisely, although reluctantly, pulls away from their lip lock.

"Listen baby, I want you as much as you want me, but this isn't the way I want you."

"Your body says different, and right now I like what its saying better."

"Don't make this harder than it has to be."

"As far as I can feel, it's much too late for that, so stop fighting and let me have it, we've waited long enough."

"Listen! I fully expect to receive all that God has for us by doing this thing the right way."

"But Marcus, I may not ever see you again, or at least have this opportunity again."

"I don't believe that and in any case, I don't want our last act together to be one of disobedience. Do you?"

"Right now I don't care."

"Let me put it to you like this; if us being together forever is a result of us doing the right thing regardless of the circumstances, then I'm going to do the right thing. I want you for a lifetime, not just for a fleeting moment where I have to get right up and leave. That's not love, it's just sex, and that's not what I want from you."

"You just had to go and get all spiritual on me and blow my groove; so, now what?"

"So now, just sit here and let me hold your fine self and take in the fragrance that is you."

"I guess I can do that."

Marcus pulls her close and holds her tight. He knows he just dodged a bullet. He wonders if she realizes how difficult that was for him, as much as he would love to be drenched in her love. He only gave her half the reasons and the only one she needed to hear. He has to focus on making it through the night. And now, while engulfed in their warm embrace, his phone rings, and it's Jackson.

"What's up Pop?"

"Marcus, me and your grandmother are about to leave, and we wanted to see you before we left. Are you at home?"

"Not yet, but I'm on my way."

"Okay, we'll see you there."

Marcus hangs up, and takes a few more minutes to hold Zephora, since the phone call robbed him of a few. Then he slowly gets up still holding her, and with her legs wrapped around his waist and her arms around his neck. She releases her legs from his waist and her arms from his neck just to wrap them around his back and place her head on his chest. They walk to the front door and Marcus takes a deep breath and lets his hands search every part of her back, continuing to her butt and then ended by gently cupping her cheeks in his hands.

"No long goodbyes baby because I'll be back before you know it. I need you to stay strong. Plan that wedding as if it's for us. Don't worry about me, and keep praying."

"I will Marcus. And you better come back 'cause I sure would hate to give all this to someone else."

"Now you know I can't let that happen."

They laugh, hug and kiss, and then Marcus slips out the door. Zephora closes and locks the door behind him, then slides down the door, sits on the floor and cries. Marcus gets in his car and pulls off watching his rear view mirror. Sure enough, they follow him. He takes the long way home to give Jackson and Ruth time to get there. Seems fitting that he should get a chance to say goodbye to them possibly for the last time. He calls Charlie; he just wanted to hear her voice. When she answers, the first thing out of his mouth is, "I love you." She responds with, "I know you do." They laugh and she informs him that she is going to the Bahamas. He is excited for her because he knows she has always wanted to go. They engage in some small talk and he tells her he'll see her when she gets back. She never suspects anything is wrong other than the obvious. They hang up and now Marcus is ready. He has said goodbye to his baby and to his sister, and next he'll get a chance to say goodbye to his grandmother. After that, he'll be ready to handle business. They say it is hard to beat a man in his own home, and Marcus is ready to show them why.

CHAPTER XX

As Marcus pulls up to his house, he notices Angelo's car across the street, however, Angelo wasn't in it and there were no lights on in his house. He hopes Kwazan's men didn't come there first and kill his friend. He backs into the driveway and before he can pull into the garage, Jackson and Ruth pull up. He sees the thugs pull up down the street, rushes over to Jackson's car and lets Ruth out. She slowly gets out and Marcus gives her a big hug, and instantly he feels like a little boy again. His grandmother's hugs always take him back to childhood. Jackson comes around the car and he and Marcus shake hands.

"We don't have a lot of time son, but we didn't want to leave without saying goodbye."

"I appreciate that, and I'm sorry I didn't get a chance to spend a lot of time with you guys."

"That's alright baby, grandma understands. You be safe and remember God can work out any situation. Now give me another hug so I can sit back down in the car."

"Thank you granny, I love you."

"I love you too baby."

Marcus helps his grandmother back into the car and then turns his attention towards Jackson. Jackson has a bewildered look on his face and Marcus knows that means he has a lot to say. They walk back around to the driver's side of the car away from Ruth's nosey ears, and Marcus addresses Jackson.

"So what's up Pop? We could have done the goodbyes over the phone."

"Son, just hear me out."

"Okay, I'm listening."

"I have something I was going to give you when you got married, but that didn't happen. I had to decide whether to wait until you did get married later, or to still give it to you."

"What is it?"

Jackson reaches in his pocket and pulls out a small black ring box. When Marcus opens the box, in it is a solid white gold ring with nine diamonds on top inside of a depressed black onyx square, the ring is huge. Eight of the diamonds are one third karat in size and are arranged with one in every corner of the square and one in the middle of each side of the square. The last diamond is in the center of the square and is one karat in size. Marcus had never seen anything like it before.

"That is a beautiful ring! Where did you get it from?"

"This, my son, is your birthright."

"My what?"

"Yes. This has been handed down in our family for generations. I have no idea how your great, great, grandfather kept this ring hidden when he was captured by slave runners and became a slave, but he did. So you see, it is not only beautiful, but also very, very old. I was told that it has been in our family for centuries, and now it belongs to you. Wear it with pride."

"Thanks pop, I will. It fits perfectly, like it was made for me. But why are you giving me a history lesson now after all this time?"

"I just wanted to give you the ring. I haven't done much right in my life by you and I wanted to make sure I did this part right. I love you and I am very proud of you and of what you've become. I didn't have a hand in guiding your life, but God raised you up just fine without me. We gotta go son, I'll call you when we get in."

"Thanks for the ring pop. You guys drive safely. I love you."

This is the first time Marcus has ever said those words to his father. Jackson has been waiting a long time to hear them, and when he did, they made him warm with joy all over. Marcus stands there and watches them pull off waving as they go down the street. As they disappear into the night, his smile changes into the fierce look of a warrior. He jumps back into his ride and backs it into the garage. He watches the garage door come down and doesn't get out of the car until it does. Then he hurries into the house to prepare for the showdown he knows is coming. He is careful not to turn on any lights and proceeds to close all of the blinds. He heads upstairs and on the way to the staircase, he trips over a shoe with a foot in it. He jumps up ready to throw down and then realizes its Angelo.

"Angelo, what are you doing here?"

"You told me to bring you the disk when I got it done, and I'll take Zephora her phone tomorrow. I knew you would probably be at Zephora's for a while, so I let myself in and fell asleep waiting on you."

"You shouldn't be here."

"Why not?"

"Kwazan's men have been following me and they are out there now and I think their planning on taking me out."

"Really? Then obviously I should be here. Finally, I get to crack some heads."

"Man you always ready to crack some heads, but this time we do it my way."

"That's fine, as long as I get to do some damage. I can't stand them fools."

"No problem, but I got a little pinned up anger to release too. Now let's go upstairs and plan our attack."

Marcus and Angelo head upstairs to set their ambush. Marcus goes in the bathroom, turns on the light, and turns the water on in the shower. Outside, Kwazan's men see the light go on and decide to make their move. They cut the wires to the alarm and pick the lock to the back door. Marcus and Angelo hear them enter and wait for them in the master bedroom. They are posted behind both sides of the double bedroom doors. They'll be able to see their attackers between the cracks in the door jams before they are noticed.

Marcus hears them coming up the stairs and his heart begins to pump hard and fast. He has had a lot of training, but never had to actually use it on anyone. His hands are sweaty and he fights to remain calm. He knows what he has to do and is ready to do it. Angelo is on the other side as cool as the other side of the pillow. The anticipation excites him, and he can't wait to unleash hell on Kwazan's men. Marcus and Angelo are armed with the weapons he keeps for their sparring sessions. They both love to use the half-staff because it feels and acts like an extension of the arm.

Kwazan's two goons are at the top of the stairs now and making their way towards the master bedroom. All Marcus can think about is Zephora. One mistake and he will never see her again. Gotta do this just right, the timing has to be perfect. Once they pass beyond the doors, strike until they stop moving. Kwazan's men creep slowly through the doorway, and just as they are about to reach the end of the doors, Marcus and Angelo are simultaneously ready to take a step forward to strike them, but before they can make their move, the two men fall face first to the floor like sacks of potatoes.

CHAPTER XXI

From behind the doors, Marcus and Angelo can see the two men lying on the floor with bullet holes in the center of their backs and the blood flowing from their lifeless bodies all over Marcus' Brazilian cherry hardwood floors. Marcus and Angelo remain perfectly still; whoever killed those men may be out to get them next. They see someone trying to step around the two dead bodies on the floor, and again get into their attack positions, when a voice rings out through the house.

"Marcus Howard! We are government agents and we're here to help you!"

The two friends are skeptical and remain in their positions. It sounded like something you would hear in a movie just before you're shot dead. With their hearts pounding and adrenaline flowing, they prepare to pounce on this new threat.

"Put down your weapons and come from behind the doors. If we wanted to hurt you, you would be dead already!"

Reluctantly, Marcus and Angelo put down their weapons and come out from behind the doors. Marcus turns on the light and fully beholds the terrible sight of Kwazan's men's lifeless bodies lying there. His house is now teaming with government agents. There were four upstairs with them, and they spoke not a word, just went about the business of going through the dead guys' pockets, putting their bodies in body bags, and cleaning up the blood on the floor with supplies they brought with them. Pretty efficient for government guys whom Marcus has no idea why they are there in the first place. And from the way they are going about their business, it looks like they don't want anyone else to know they were ever there. Downstairs there were at least two more agents. Marcus and Angelo weave their way through the bodies, both dead and alive, and head downstairs.

"Marcus, what kind of super spy mess have you gotten me into?

"Your guess is as good as mine, but I'm sure we will soon find out."

By the time they make it downstairs, a car pulls into the driveway, and a tall very distinguished older gentleman gets out. By his demeanor, it was easy to see that he was in charge. The downstairs agents forcefully direct Marcus and Angelo to the couch. They involuntarily take a seat looking like two little boys who have been sent to the principal's office. One agent stood on both sides of the couch. There were a total of six agents in the house already; the two who were following Marcus, the two who were following Kwazan's now dead guards, and two who are driving a van for the disposal of the dead bodies. Together, these three teams coordinated the surprise attack of Kwazan's guards and ultimately resolved the situation before Marcus and Angelo could make their move. Angelo was a little disturbed because he missed yet another opportunity to bash in a few heads. Marcus, on the other hand, was relieved. Although he was ready to take a life if he needed to, he really had no desire to do so. He believes in trying to work things out through diplomacy, however, this was just not one of those times.

As the lead agent walks in with a stern look on his face, Marcus and Angelo turn and look at each other in anticipation of what was coming next.

"Are you two gentlemen alright?"

"Yes we're fine, but do you mind telling us what just happened here?"

"Well Mr. Howard, we have been following these two men for some time now. They are responsible for at least one murder and it looks like you two were next on their list. Lucky for you we were on to them."

"We appreciate your help, but we had everything under control, and probably would have resolved this thing without the loss of life."

"Listen, I know you think you could have handled it, but those guys are highly trained assassins. What happened here is part of an ongoing investigation, you can't mention it to anyone."

"I don't know about any investigation, but I do know who those two worked for and I'm sure when they don't come back, he will send more."

"Fortunately as we speak, we have agents at Kwazan's hotel questioning him about his business here in the states. He has a full staff with him, but only brought those two assassins with him for protection. When they don't show up, he will know they are dead, and hopefully he will decide to do his business on the up and up."

"Okay, so who are you and how do you know Kwazan?"

"Who I am is unimportant, and I told you this is an ongoing investigation. We can't touch him because he is a diplomat, but I am glad we were able to neutralize the threat to you. Why do you think he was after you anyway?"

"I'm not sure, maybe because I am about to start doing business in Africa."

"Okay. My men will remain here and finish cleanup here, and then they will fade into the neighborhood like they were before this happened. There will always be two of them watching your back at all times until this investigation is complete. You probably won't see them, just know they are there for your protection."

Why? Why do I still need protecting?"

"You know, you ask a lot of questions, and my response will continue to be…

"Yeah, I know, part of an ongoing investigation."

"Exactly, you catch on fast. I must leave you now. Remember, not a word to anyone, and thank you for serving your country."

"Sure, whatever, but can we go about our normal schedule? My business will be taking me out of the country soon, and will your men be going with me?"

"Again with the questions; as long as your passport is in order, feel free to handle your business as you normally would. Just know, you now have government issued protection, and hopefully that should help you sleep better at night. Good night gentlemen."

The lead agent leaves as silently as he arrived. The other agents continue their cleanup efforts, and when Marcus' house looks the way it did before they arrived, they leave as well and disappear into the night. Marcus goes into the kitchen and pulls out a bottle of V.S.O.P. Hennessey, and a couple of glasses and pours he and Angelo a drink, and then another, and another. The two friends have been through a lot together, but this was a first. And with every trial they face, the two become better friends and more trusting of one another, if that is possible.

"You know Marcus, as much as I was ready, willing and able to take those guys out, I'm sure glad we didn't have to."

"Yeah, me too, but you know what, there is no one else on this planet I would rather go into battle with than you. I love you man."

"I love you too brotha. Now I hope you got clean sheets on the bed in the guest room, because I'm drunk, and I need to go to sleep."

"Your room is always ready. Don't fall down the stairs, I ain't got no insurance."

Marcus locks all the doors downstairs and makes his way to his room. The bodies are gone and so are the blood stains. He pulls off his clothes, throws them on the floor and jumps into bed. The pillows and sheets are drenched with Zephora's scent. He hugs his pillow like a person, takes a big sniff of her enchanting aroma and begins to drift off to sleep.

"Zephora, I love you with all my heart."

CHAPTER XXII

Marcus has made it through the drama. Now he is able to rest easy through the night with his thoughts and heart fixed on Zephora. For the next few days, Marcus and Angelo work on getting Angelo up to speed in the business. And just as they had predicted years ago, the two of them work together beautifully. The cohesiveness they share as friends transcended into business and has created a perfect harmony. Marcus taught and Angelo learned. For the next week, the two are inseparable helping to keep Marcus' mind off Zephora, only taking breaks to eat and sleep.

Angelo is the perfect match for the business. His aptitude for the business is astounding, and his personality gives strength to the other employees. Not strength greater than what Marcus has always provided them through his encouragement, just different and in its own way more empowering. With the employees invested, their production rate increases. And when Angelo finds the time, he spends it with Veronica. Marcus is pleased and he knows he can leave now and everything will be alright. He is all smiles on the outside, but inside, his heart is weeping. He misses Zephora terribly. The best way to end his misery is to accomplish his mission. Tonight Marcus will be on the phone getting his itinerary together. Angelo is ready to step in and Marcus is ready to put an end to Kwazan's tyranny.

Zephora is finally able to bring her mother home. Saphera's condition has improved with every passing day and there is no sign of the virus in her body. Now Saphera has a new fight, a fight to restore her estranged relationship with her daughter. She has learned a valuable lesson; however, regaining lost trust is much harder than losing it. Nevertheless, it has to be Saphera's first priority. After that, she will be able to focus on the Kwazan problem. Now that Zephora has the papers from the safety deposit box, it's time to sit down and discuss them.

Zephora hasn't had much to say since Marcus has been torn from her life. She has to return to work soon and has no idea how she will function. She sometimes has regrets about signing those papers, however she knows that would have cost her mother's life and Kwazan would have still pursued his conquest. She has no desire for her mother to die, even though she feels betrayed by her. Zephora loves her mother and really doesn't want anything to happen to her; she has already lost one parent to this madness. Zephora finds herself now in never land. Never thought she would have to give up the love of her life to save her mother's life, never thought her mother would lie to her about anything or keep such life changing information from her, never thought she was the queen of anything other than her own life, and never in a million years thought she would be a part of an arranged marriage. All of that gives Zephora new meaning to the words, "never say never."

Life is so funny. One day you can be on top of the world, and the next day it can feel as though the world is on top of you. Marcus and Zephora are finding out that life is rippled with all kinds of twists and turns, and no one can predict what will happen next. They are earning a new respect for life in all its forms. It's not just the highs that make up a good life, but also the lows and how you respond to them. It seems the way to navigate through all the waves of emotions is to just give in to them and ride them out. Not give up, but give in.

Fighting to not encounter any lows in life will keep you from experiencing any of the highs. The two are connected and must be given the same respect. All that Marcus and Zephora have and are experiencing thus far is shaping them into better equipped individuals; individuals who have dealt with loss and disappointment and know how to get through it. No one knows what the future holds, however, as hard as it may be, all they can do is accept the good and the bad, hold

160

their heads up high, opens their hearts and minds and experience the whole ride; the blissfulness of the highs, the anguish of the lows, and the peace when things are on level ground, without regret. Just like a rollercoaster, life can take your breath away. You have to be prepared to accept the whole ride; the anticipation of reaching the top, the screams when the bottom drops, and then, when the ride is over, you want to do it all over again because you willingly gave in to the ups and the downs.

Once Zephora can get past feeling sorry for herself, she will be ready for the next new experience. Her problem is she has lost her anchors; her mother, whom she can't stand right now, and Marcus, who is always able to inspire her. Some challenges she must face alone. It will cause her to reach inside herself and dig deeper than she ever has before; and as a queen to be, this is a quality she needs to harness.

It's late in the night, and Zephora has spent another day sulking and feeling sorry for herself. Her already weak self-esteem is now dragging in the dirt. Just as she is about to turn out the light and cry herself to sleep, Zephora receives a text message. *"My Love, stop feeling sorry for yourself. With every step we take, we get closer to the finish line of life and this ordeal. So stop dragging your feet and holding your head*

161

down and take steps of victory and we will have it. Smile, know I am there and get up and do your part. ☺."

Marcus knows her oh so well, and he can feel she is contemplating giving up. Even though he can't physically be there, he found a way to be there spiritually and emotionally instead. His words of motivation have resonated in Zephora's heart and soul. Tonight she will sleep peacefully, and tomorrow she will wake up a renewed person and ready to meet her challenges head on.

PART 5

BLOOD, SWEAT & TEARS

CHAPTER XXIII

Charlie and Mr. Netumba have finally made it to the Bahamas. Mr. Netumba made reservations at one of the islands best resorts and Charlie is having the time of her life. While she is lounging, taking in the sun, ordering in and people watching (mostly men), Mr. Netumba is out investigating the island and its inhabitants trying to find the answers he is looking for. His agenda is more work than pleasure, and he is pretty determined to discover what he has been searching years to find.

One day, after lounging by the pool, Charlie went back to her room and pulled out the information her father had given her. Play time is over, and it is now time to find out why Mr. Netumba had brought her there and why her father had given her those papers. She took a shower and got dressed, then knocked on Mr. Netumba's door and got no response as usual; he always seemed to be out somewhere. She decided to call a cab and go alone to the address on the paperwork she received from Jackson. When she arrived at the address, it turned out to be a business. The sign above the door read *Babwean Imports, Established in 1761.*

As Charlie stands in front of the door and prepares to knock, she has butterflies in the pit of her stomach. She is extremely nervous, her arm pits and hands are sweating and she has no idea what to expect. Reluctantly she knocks on the door, and when the door opens, she gets the shock of her life. She is greeted by an elderly woman whose face closely resembled her own.

"Ma'am, my father gave me this information and told me to seek out the owner of this establishment."

"Good day, I am the owner, I am Madam Zigumba."

"Hello Madam Zigumba, my name is Charlie Howard and I'm here to present you with this paperwork and hopefully you can tell me what it all means."

"Come in baby and let me see what you have here."

Charlie goes inside and is directed to a big office at the end of the hall. Once there, she is surprised to see Mr. Netumba sitting in the office. As comfortable as he looks, it seems he has been there a while already.

"What are you doing here," Charlie asks.

"Me? What about you?

"My father gave me some papers and told me to come here."

"Really? Why didn't you tell me about that?"

"I didn't think it was any of your business. Now you still haven't told me why you're here."

"I'm here to get answers to some lifelong questions. Oddly enough, my search was prompted by you and your wedding gift to your brother. I was hoping to get the information and bring it back to you, but it would seem that is not necessary now, seeing that you are here all on your own."

"I'm here because my father sent me, but what does this place and Madam Zigumba have to do with you and your search?"

"I guess we will both find that out together in a minute."

Mr. Netumba knows full well the connection; however, he wants Charlie to find out on her own. Madam Zigumba sat in front of her and reads the information that Charlie has provided. After which, with a look that could best be described as joyful astonishment, she excuses herself from the office and goes to a room at the other end of the hall. Charlie and

Mr. Netumba are puzzled by her confusing response to the information. Simultaneously, they both look at each other and shrug their shoulders with bewilderment. When Madam Zigumba returns to the office, she is carrying a briefcase that is so thick with dust that it emits a cloud of dust that follows her from the other room and all the way down the hall to the office. The cloud is so thick that it causes Charlie and Mr. Netumba to cough and sneeze. She laid the briefcase on her desk and more dust flies into the air and engulfs the room like a dense fog over a lake on a cool morning. Mr. Netumba pulls a handkerchief out of his pocket and covers his nose, while Charlie, who is not so prepared, uses her hand to feebly try and fan away the dust. Madam Zigumba, seemingly immune to the dust, casually takes a seat in her big burgundy leather executive desk chair with solid brass rivets and starts to speak.

"I apologize for all the dust, but this case has not been moved for many, many years. You have both come here looking for answers. I have waited a long time for someone to come asking the right questions. I was about to give up hope that anyone would ever come, but as I know all too well, God answers prayers in His own time. My husband and I had no children so my bloodline ends with me. You, Charlie, have come to me with a face that looks like mine as if you are my very own child. And you, Zuri, have come to me with knowledge of ancient times and language I haven't heard since the days of my grandfather. The fact that you two came to this island together and both found your way here separately is amazing and has restored this old lady's faith. Charlie, when you leave this island, take this briefcase with you; however, do not open it until you are on a plane to your next destination."

"What next destination?"

"Zuri will fill you in on that later. For now, just know that this briefcase is yours to keep. And once you open it, you have the authority to do whatever you like with what you find in it."

"Madam Zigumba, you are just going to give it to her just like that?" Mr. Netumba asks.

Madam Zigumba sits back in her chair, props her arms on the arms of her chair and slowly crosses her legs. Her desk is made of glass and as she crosses her legs, her dress is pulled up over the calf of her leg revealing an oddly shaped, dark colored birth mark on her right leg. Charlie immediately notices it, and her eyes grow to an enormously large size upon seeing the distinctive mark on Madam Zigumba's leg, and she blurts out "Oh my God!"

"Whatever is wrong my dear?"

"My brother and I both have that same birth mark on our right legs too. It is so distracting that I am ashamed when I where shorts or short skirts or short dresses."

"You have a brother?"

"Yes and he has an import/export business much like this one; not quite this big, but successful just the same."

"Amazing, is he your only brother?"

"Yes, why?"

"Well my dear, the answer to that question is in the briefcase. Now, no more questions, let me show you around my business, and later, you two must join me for dinner. I have one of the finest chefs on this island."

Charlie and Zuri both agree to stay without any reservations, hoping to pump the old lady for more information. In one afternoon, Madam Zigumba's whole world and her mood has changed. Her voice has excitement in it as she meticulously shows them (mainly Charlie) the ins and outs of her establishment. The business is over 200 years old and if that isn't enough to say, it employs over 300 people; not to mention, she also owns two large cargo ships. Babwean Imports is one of the oldest and largest import/export businesses in the Caribbean. Charlie is overwhelmed by its size and grandeur, yet empowered by the fact that it is owned and operated by Madam Zigumba.

After the tour, the three of them take a limo to the Zigumba mansion. It is a fifty acre estate right on the beach. The mansion itself is a 20,000 square foot marvel of handcrafted workmanship. Behind it is a junior Olympic size covered and heated pool, and a private beach. Charlie has a hard time keeping her bottom lip off the floor. As they tour the mansion, each room they enter is seemingly more magnificent than the one before it. Madam Zigumba insists that they check out of the resort and come and stay with her for the remainder of their trip. Both Charlie and Zuri happily accept and are beside themselves with excitement. The three new friends eat dinner on a balcony overlooking the beach while being served hand and foot by the mansions courteous and pleasant staff. The evening is kissed by a slight breeze that carries a tropical fragrance to the unsuspecting nostrils of the mansion guests. As they watch the sun beyond the waters and listen to the soothing sounds of the waves rushing back and forth, a sense of total relaxation grips Charlie and Zuri as they enjoy dinner and great conversation by candlelight and light Caribbean jazz playing in the background.

It's morning, Zuri and Charlie pack their bags and take Madam Zigumba's limo back to the mansion. For the remainder of their trip they will stay at the mansion as special guests of Madam Zigumba to be waited on tirelessly by the mansion staff. It is far better than the resort or any five star hotel, and much more than either of them could have ever expected. Madam Zigumba becomes very fond of Charlie and takes the time to show her more about the business. Charlie, who has always been an excellent student, soaks up everything like a sponge. By the end of the week, Charlie is running things. Madam Zigumba proudly sits back and watches her work, taking the time to insert some leadership tips every now and then. She is amazed at how instinctive it all seems to Charlie. She has tried to show others how to run the business, but none were able to handle the pressures of managing people and product like Charlie.

While Charlie is learning how to be a business mogul, Zuri takes the time to check in on his various projects. He makes sure Saphera and Zephora are in good hands with their wedding planning, and then he checks in on Marcus, who has booked and taken his flight to Africa and is having no further interference from Kwazan. He also has found out from his contacts that Kwazan is laying low. Although Kwazan is having Saphera and Zephora watched, he allows them to do their shopping and planning uninterrupted. Everything seems to be going smoothly, so Zuri decides to actually allow himself to relax. It is the first time in a long time he totally lets his guard down and kicks back, and it feels good.

The time eventually comes for them to leave, but they have fallen in love with the island, the mansion, and the service and don't want to go. Like spoiled little children they slowly pack their bags one piece at a time. Hours later, members of the staff carry their bags to the limo which has been waiting for several hours to be loaded. Charlie has tears in her eyes as she comes downstairs to say her goodbyes. She and Madam Zigumba have bonded and formed a friendship that is certainly unexpected. Charlie gives Madam Zigumba a comforting long hug and vows she will return. Madam Zigumba hands Charlie an envelope full of cash as payment for the work she had done in the business. Charlie refuses to take it, but Madam Zigumba insists and will not take no for an answer.

Zuri expresses his eternal gratitude for her hospitality and Madam Zigumba humbly expresses what an honor it was to get to know him. Hugs, kisses and tears fill the foyer, and then the two travelers get into the limo and are off to the airport. Zuri has already taken the time to change their travel arrangements and is pleased with the way things have turned out, but is apprehensive about the next leg of their journey. On the way to the airport, the phone in the car rings and the driver lets down the privacy glass and lets Charlie know it is for her.

"Hello?"

"Charlie my dear?"

"Yes Madam Zigumba."

"I couldn't let you leave the island without telling you something."

"What would that be ma'am?"

"Just so you know, all the members of my family for seven hundred years have been born with that birth mark on their right leg. So I would appreciate it if you would call me Aunt Sophie from now on."

"Excuse me!?"

"That's right child, now have a nice flight and I will talk to you later."

"In that case, I suppose it would be okay for me to say I love you Aunt Sophie?"

"I love you too child. Bye."

Tears of joy and excitement began to run down Charlie's face as she hangs up the phone. This trip is much more than she ever expected and it all is a little overwhelming to her.

"What's up?" Mr. Netumba asks.

"I just gained an aunt."

"Well, she's a great one to have."

"Somehow I think you knew this already."

"What are you talking about?"

"Yeah, right, okay. So Zuri, I mean Mr. Netumba, where in the world are we off to now?"

"Next stop, Africa!"

CHAPTER XXIV

While Charlie and Mr. Netumba were in the Bahamas, Marcus was on his own journey afar. He had many concerns about his trip; however, none of them over shadowed his reason for going. How could he just hand over the woman of his dreams, his soul mate, and his best friend to a murderous madman like Kwazan? He couldn't, thus no matter what trials he may encounter, no matter what obstacles he had to hurdle, and no matter where he had to go, and he had to give a 125% effort to keep her safe and away from Kwazan.

Marcus tries to pack enough clothes for an extended stay in Africa since he has no idea how long it will take to accomplish his goal. Of course this means two to three changes of clothes for every day. What Marcus calls two weeks of preparation, is what other people call a month of preparation. He stuffs everything he can in two large pieces of luggage, one medium piece of luggage and one carry-on luggage that is still filled to capacity just like the rest of them. Right before boarding the plane, Marcus takes the time to send Zephora a text message. *"On my way Ze. Luv ya"* She quickly responds back with one of her own. *"Be careful baby. I love you back."*

This is going to be the longest trip Marcus has ever taken. "Hopefully I can establish some business relationships while I'm here and make my business internationally known," he thought to himself. His flight is long but smooth the entire way. And after such a long flight, Marcus is glad to be back on solid ground. The moment he passes through the gate, he immediately sends Zephora another text letting her know he has arrived safely, and she responds with a smiley face and a kiss.

Marcus is on a budget and needs to conserve his funds, so he makes reservations in a two star hotel. He can't help but notice the two agents who are watching over him, even though they are supposed to be invisible, as he checks in. He does however feel safe as long as he knows they are there. Maybe he will have a trouble free trip with them here, just maybe. Before Marcus left the States, he bought a solid 14 carat gold rope chain to put his father's ring on. The ring is pretty big and he doesn't want to wear it on his finger because it might attract too much attention. So he decides to wear it underneath his clothing around his neck. When Marcus gets to his room, he is sorely surprised at what a two star hotel means in Malawi, Africa, but he has no choice but to deal with it; at least it doesn't have roaches.

It is still early once Marcus gets settled in so he decides to take a walking tour of Malawi's capital city. He is amazed to see that even half way around the world, things are the same; the rich on the north side of the city and the poor on the south. The disparity between rich and poor is a worldwide experience and here it is even more prevalent. As Marcus experiences what true poverty is, he begins to weep for the people and vows to do what he can to help them by building his business to the international level, hiring the poor disenfranchised people and sending what he can to help these poverty stricken people.

The next day Marcus takes a trip to the ruins of the Great Zimbabwe. It is a three day journey there. Always close behind him, are the two agents, who are assigned to keep him safe. The ruins are magnificent. He has never seen anything like it before. He walks the entire area touching the wall every chance he gets trying to connect with the past. Back in the area said to have housed the city's royal and noble families, Marcus notices patterns in the wall. One of the patterns seems to match the configuration of his father's ring. Marcus is astounded and immediately takes pictures of the patterns to be able to compare them later. He keeps walking until he reaches the top of the hill. From there, he is able to look over the entire valley. As he stands there, a warm and invigorating breeze engulfs the area. As the breeze rushes through the area, Marcus spreads his arms out wide to experience the full effect of the gentle wind. A chill goes up Marcus' spine as he hears a whisper in his ear as the wind pushes passed him. The whisper sounds as if it is riding the wind. The whispering voice says *"Home"* and Marcus quickly turns to see who is behind him, but there is no one there.

Marcus is definitely spooked and decides that it is time to go. Still in shock about what he heard, Marcus is more than ready for his three day trip back. Without anyone to bounce the experience off of, Marcus has to keep it to himself. Once he gets back to Lilongwe and shakes off the ghosts, Marcus decides to spend the next couple of days sampling some of the country's fine cuisine before he takes the four and a half day trip to the Lost City of Mapungubwe.

The afternoon before he is set to leave on his next journey, while he is dining, a man dressed in a royal manner, spots Marcus dining alone. Marcus is wearing white linen pants with a black linen shirt that has a wide collar and a deep V-cut that ends at the bottom of his well-defined pectoral muscles. His father's ring hangs right in the middle of the V in his shirt and catches the light every time Marcus moves. The man gets up from his table and approaches Marcus.

Mr. Netumba's men are several tables behind Marcus, but are aware of the man approaching and are on high alert. The man notices the two men out of the corner of his eye, but acts as if he doesn't. He proceeds to sit down at Marcus' table and introduces himself.

"How are you today sir? My name is Zuka Tsimba."

"How's it going? I'm Marcus, what can I do for you?"

"I have noticed you here in town over the past week or so. Are you a tourist or are you here on business?"

"Why, what's it to you?"

"I'm sorry sir, I didn't mean to intrude or offend you. I was merely curious."

"Both, but if you don't mind, I would like to finish my meal…alone."

"Sorry sir, but if I may, one more question please?"

"Okay, what is it?"

"I couldn't help but notice the beautiful ring around your neck. How and where did you come in possession of such a beautiful ring?"

"It belongs to my father. Do you recognize it?"

"Yes, my family has one very similar to it."

"Really? Maybe you can help me out then?"

"How sir?"

"Do you know of a man named Kwazan Tshuma?"

"But of course. He is one of the royal noblemen here of our ruling tribal council and will be king. But how do you know him?"

"Never mind that, but I must speak to the ruling council at once on a matter of the utmost importance. Can you take me to them?"

"I myself am a part of the ruling council. What information do you have?"

"I would rather talk with the whole council please."

"Okay. Come to this address in the morning and it will all be arranged."

Zuka writes an address down for Marcus and gets up and leaves in a rush. Once out of Marcus' line of sight, he pulls out his phone and makes a call.

"Hello Kwazan? He is here. You want him dead or detained?"

"Thank you Zuka my friend. I want him just detained for now, but give him my warmest welcome to my country."

"Okay Kwazan. Did you find her?"

"Yes and she is beautiful. We are to be wed in about thirty days, and Zuka?"

"Yes what is it?"

"Watch out for the two watching him. They need not be detained."

"I have already seen them and they will be dealt with first."

"Thank you Zuka. I will see you in about thirty days."

"Always a pleasure to serve you Kwazan, my king," Zuka states proudly.

The next morning Marcus got up excited and ready to go. Finally he is going to get the answers he is looking for. He goes downstairs and has breakfast. He asks his waitress if she knows where the address is and she gives him directions to the location. For that, he gives her a little extra in the tip. It is a beautiful day so Marcus decides to walk and not far behind him are his protectors. His directions are pretty easy, go two blocks, turn left, go two blocks, turn right, and it's the second building on the left. He makes his first left, but before his protectors can make the turn, a van cuts them off and they are shoved into the van by four men with automatic weapons. Once in the van, their hands are bound behind their backs and it speeds off. They are told to sit down and then the van slows and the four gunmen jump out the back. Mr. Netumba's men watch as the man in the front passenger seat of the van screws a silencer onto his 9mm handgun. They turn and look at one another, nod their heads to each other, and then, two silent shots and Netumba's men are dead, both shot execution style in the head. The driver and passenger drive the van to the poorest part of the city and get out. They walk about fifty feet from the van and it explodes.

All Mr. Netumba's men have locator beacons. As long as they are alive the beacons are silent. So when the two locators start to beep, Mr. Netumba knows he has a problem. He pulls his locating device out of his pocket to see who is in trouble, and realizes that it's his men in Africa. He and Charlie are in route there, but won't be there for several hours. Then the beeps stop and disappear off the screen. Mr. Netumba reaches for the air phone and makes a call.

"Hey, I'm calling in a favor. Two of my men are dead in Africa. I know you have a Seal team training there and......."

"Say no more. I'll let them know you are coming."

"Thanks General, I really appreciate it."

"No problem, I owe you. And Colonel, I'm sorry for your loss. I know how much your men mean to you."

"Thanks General, but I still have an important stray lost down there and I have to get him out."

"Good luck Colonel."

Mr. Netumba hangs up the phone and Charlie, who is half asleep, turns over.

What's going on, who was that?"

"Just my men checking in, go back to sleep.

Charlie turns back over and Mr. Netumba bows his head and says a prayer for his men and then says one for Marcus.

"Hang on Marcus, help is on the way."

Marcus is unaware of what just happened and continues his trek, but before he can make his next turn, a second van stops and subdues him. They place a black sack over his head and bind his arms behind his back. Marcus' heart is pounding so hard it feels as though it will come through his chest, but he tries to remains calm and says nothing. Surely the agents will rescue him soon.

"Your guards are dead; no one will be coming for you now."

Panic tries to grip Marcus, but somehow he keeps his wits about him. The van stops and he is taken from the van.

They take him into a building and down an elevator. They go down what seems to be four floors, Marcus hears the door open and then he is shoved out. No one else gets out of the elevator and the door closes and goes back up. His head is still covered and Marcus is lying on the floor when he hears footsteps coming his way. He struggles to get to his feet and get his bearings. As he does, someone uncovers his head and he opens his eyes to a nightmare. He is surrounded by eight men with machine guns dressed in brown military fatigues. He looks around to view his surroundings. He sees a long hall with eight cells on both sides. Each cell has a steel door with a sliding four by four opening for looking out and one that looks like it is for feeding purposes. The men escort him to the other end of the hall into a big empty space with only a water hose in it, and cut the ties off his arms.

"Okay, buddy, strip."

"Why am I here?"

"I will not ask again, now strip!"

"Why am I here?"

The soldier shoves the butt of his gun into Marcus' stomach and Marcus falls to his knees gasping for air.

185

"Strip now!"

Marcus takes off his clothes down to his underwear and t-shirt and throw them in the corner.

"Everything!!"

Marcus slowly takes off the rest of his clothing, and then one of the soldiers directs him to stand against the wall. One of the others grabs the hose and sprays Marcus down. The force of the water is so powerful that it thrust Marcus against the wall. It takes all his strength to cover his private area with his hands. They turn off the water, tell him to turn around, and repeat the process on his back side. After hosing him down, they place shackles on his ankles and walk the battered naked man down the hall to the last cell on the left and shove him in and lock the door.

"I don't know what you did and I don't care, but whatever it was had to be bad. This place has not been used for years and you are the only one here now."

"Listen, I am an American citizen and I have done nothing wrong."

"Someone will be here later to bring you food. We feed you twice a day and we don't let you out for exercise. Enjoy your stay."

"Wait! You can't do this to me, I've done nothing wrong!"

Marcus hears them laugh as they walk away, and then he hears the outer door close, then the lights go out and the elevator goes up and Marcus realizes he is all alone now. His would be protectors are dead; his best friend is on the other side of the world, his woman is about to marry his new found enemy and he is powerless to do anything about it. He's been stripped naked and left to rot in a cold dark hole, and no one knows where he is. The cell has a toilet, a dirty mattress, a pillow, and one blanket. He uses the blanket to wrap around his naked body and tries to get warm. It stinks, but at this point it doesn't matter. He gets in his bunk and leans against the wall with his knees pulled close to his chest. The only light he has is coming from the one in the hall and it flickers off and on every couple of minutes. He puts his head in his hands and starts to chant.

"God will not put more on you than you can handle, God will not put more on you than you can handle, God will not put more on you than you can handle!"

"I will not die in here, I will not die in here, I will not die in here!"

"God please let someone come for me, please."

"Ze, I love you baby." Marcus whispers softly to himself.

CHAPTER XXV

Love can be and is supposed to be a truly amazing and wondrous experience. When you are truly in love with a person, heart, mind, body and soul, and that person is truly in love with you, you are able to sense how each other is feeling because true love permeates through every fiber of your being and transcends time, space and distance. Because the bond between Marcus and Zephora is so unbreakable, she senses what Marcus is going through. No, she doesn't know exactly what's going on, just that something is very wrong. She is unable to call or text him unless he calls her first. For the first time since he left, she is starting to feel helpless especially since she has no idea where he is or what he is doing, and it's driving her crazy.

"Mother, something is very wrong."

"What is it baby? You don't like the color scheme? We can change it."

"No, it's not that. Something is wrong with Marcus. I can't explain it, but I know that he's in trouble."

"I understand. I was the same way about your father. The night of the accident, I could feel it deep in my spirit.

When they called to tell me what happened, I wasn't at all surprised, just devastated because it was like confirmation of what I was already feeling. But you know, I always had the feeling that he is still here with me. And seeing him in the hospital, gave me new hope."

"Don't start that again mother. Daddy has been dead a long time and people don't just rise up from the dead you know."

"Yeah, tell that to Lazarus."

Saphera has successfully gotten Zephora's mind off of worrying about Marcus. It is the only way she can help her daughter because she has no idea what else to do.

"Anyway mother, tell me why you never remarried?"

"You only have one true love in this life, and Zuri is mine. No one else could ever compare to him or possibly provide for me and you the way he did. If I close my eyes and think about it, I can still feel his touch. It was both strong and soothing at the same time."

"Sounds magical. What am I going to do if something has happened to Marcus and he can't find a way out of this arranged marriage for us? I can't, I won't marry Kwazan. He is a vengeful, spiteful, murderous man."

"I hate that you two agreed to this madness without discussing it with me first."

"Umm, hello, you were about to die and it was the only way to save your life."

"But Zephora, you didn't have to…"

"No buts. Marcus and I agreed and there was no way we were going to let you die unnecessarily for us."

"Zephora, I don't know what to say."

"Don't say anything, it's over and done with now. And if we had to do it all over again, the decision would still be the same."

Silence consumes the room. Saphera is again touched by her daughter's actions. She could have prevented all of this if she had just told Zephora the truth about her birthright. Now, her daughter is in pain and it's all her fault and she has no way of solving the problem. The weight on her heart is so heavy that it causes tears to stream down her face. Zephora sees that her mother is crying and immediately stops what she is doing. She embraces her mother and the two of them hug long and tightly, both crying. Reconciliation is happening and Saphera is relieved. Nothing means more to her than her daughter.

Charlie and Mr. Netumba are only a few hours away from their destination. Mr. Netumba is more worried than he has ever been before. He knows that Marcus is in grave danger and he is hoping that his captors have not taken his life. Netumba's men were successful in breaking into Marcus' room and putting a homing device in his belt before all the trouble began, but from this distance, Netumba is unable to track him yet. He is helpless until they hit the ground. To help ease his mind a little, he decides to wake Charlie and have her open the briefcase she received from Madam Zigumba.

"Charlie, wake up. It's time to open the case."

"What?"

"The case, it's time to open it."

"Okay yeah, let's see what's in this thing."

Charlie reaches down and pulls the case from under her seat, sits it on her lap and slowly opens it. She has already taken the effort to clean the rest of the dust from the outside of the case, and hopes that there is no more inside. To their surprise, everything inside the case is orderly. Every document, no matter how old, has been carefully laminated to protect them from the elements. Some of the pages are so old that they were written in an old African dialect, but an English translation accompanied them.

Once she starts reading them, she finds they told the same story that Kwazan had told to Marcus, except there were a few differences. There is one laminated page that is an old scroll that showed in detail the names of the original eight families who created the Tribal Laws. As she studies over that page, she notices that one of the names of the original eight is Netumba.

"Hey, wait a minute, your name is on this scroll. If Kwazan is telling the truth about Zephora, what does that make you?"

"About Zephora, he is telling the truth. And I am actually her father."

"What!? Not possible, he died years ago."

"Supposedly, but they never found my body. And that's because I'm right here."

"Why the hell are you just now telling me this and why haven't you let her know?"

"It is too dangerous, and to really make a difference, I had to find the descendants of the other original family."

"So how did you survive and where have you been?"

"Just finish reading the information; we can talk about this later."

"I wish I might. You owe me an explanation, and I ain't reading nothing else until I get it!"

"Okay fine, but I'll keep it brief. I have been a government secret agent for years. I knew those guys were after me and my father. I was unable to get to him in time, but I managed to fool them into thinking I was in that car when it crashed. And I thought they didn't know about Saphera and Zephora so if I disappeared they would be safe. So because I was technically dead, the government was able to send me on missions that they couldn't send anyone else on. That is how no one knew about me and how I found out they knew about Zephora. When she decided to marry Marcus, I had to find out who he was and when you did your ancestry search, certain things in it gave me cause for suspicion."

"Well that explains why you knew so much about me and my brother and about my wedding gift."

"Why did you choose a gift like that anyway?"

"My brother has always wanted to know about our family history, so I got with my father and researched our family as far back as I could. We were able to go back as far as slavery which is how we got the last name of Howard."

"Do you know what it was before that?"

Charlie reaches into her purse and pulls out an envelope that has their family tree paperwork in it. She has taken great pride in putting the whole thing together for Marcus.

"Let me see, here it is. Our great, great, grandfather's name was Dakarai Sakara."

"That's interesting. You did a great job. Now that I have given you an explanation, can we get back to the scrolls now?"

Charlie goes back to researching the scrolls and as her eyes get midway down the page, she screams out.

"Oh my God!! Sakara is on this scroll too as an original family!"

"Finally!"

"You knew this all the time didn't you?"

"I had my suspicions. But I didn't put it all together until I met with Madam Zigumba. You had done so much research into your family history I wanted to take you along with me. Now you can learn the real reason behind Kwazan's take over."

"I'm listening."

"Your family was to be put to death centuries ago because one of your ancestors intercepted a scroll outlining the plot to assassinate the leader and his family of that century. There was another affluent noble family that thought they should be a part of the inner circle. The name of that family was Tshuma. The Tshuma family had two accomplices that also wanted them in the loop. One accomplice was the Tsimba family of the Mapungubwean tribe, which is my tribe, and the other accomplice was the Nyagumba family of the Zimbabwean tribe, which is your tribe. Your ancestor came to one of my ancestors and the Nyagumba family to report what he had stumbled across. Well, because we had a traitor in our mist, the news got back to the Tshumas and they focused their attention on your family and branded them traitors and won their seat on the council. Our families were friends. So we helped your family escape execution in the middle of the night with as much of their wealth as they could carry. My ancestor sent one of our trusted family aides with them. His name was Garai Zigumba. Half of the scroll with the plot on it has been in the possession of my family and the other half with your family. But because my family knew about the plot and wouldn't be bought off, we were branded co-conspirers and were supposed to be assassinated. They managed to also escape and have been on the run ever since."

"Wow, what a story!"

"There's more."

"What?"

"The council, after letting the Tshumas fill the spot vacated by your family, decided not to replace our family on the council. However, this is my families ruling century. That is why Kwazan's father got my father and me to sign the agreement in the event I had a daughter. But even more compelling is the fact that it is your family's ruling century as well, if the truth can be revealed."

"Are your trying to tell me that my brother is the rightful ruling leader?"

"Exactly, but Kwazan doesn't know about your family history. Surely it is the only reason Marcus has not been killed."

"What do you mean? Is my brother in trouble?"

"Hopefully not. But more importantly right now is the other half of the scroll with the plot on it. I hope it's in that briefcase, it is our only proof."

"Is this it?"

"Yes, thank God. With this we can restore honor to both our family names."

"If anything happens to my brother because of all of this cloak and dagger stuff, you are going to need more than your family honor."

"I have the situation under control."

"Oh, so he is in trouble?"

"Yes, but I have a team ready to go as soon as we land."

"Don't ever lie to me again. None of this crap is worth my brother's life, and it wouldn't even be happening if you would have just come clean from the beginning."

"I know and I'm sorry, but I am doing everything I can to get him back."

"You better!"

Charlie stops talking to Mr. Netumba and goes back to reading the papers in the briefcase. As she is fumbling through them, she comes across a letter that had been written at least 175 years ago. She pulls the letter out and begins to read it.

My name is Japera Sakara Zigumba. Me and my family have been exiled from our home land for a crime we did not commit. My father started a fishing and import business here on this island. Ten days ago my brothers, Dakarai, and Katura sailed to the north to trade our goods. The people there captured my brother Dakarai, and my bother Katura escaped. He died a few days ago from his wounds, but not before telling us that white skinned people had taken Dakarai prisoner. My father was very upset after losing one son and the other one dying, that it broke his heart. Yesterday he went to sleep and never woke up again. I am all that is left of my family here. I pray Dakarai is alive and can make it back home someday. The year is 1825 and me and my husband are going to continue running my father's business in hopes my brother will come back and claim his birth right.

Charlie finished the letter, placed it back in the briefcase and closed it. She pushed it back under the seat, and then leaned back in her chair with tears streaming down her face, and said a silent prayer for Marcus. *"God please protect my brother and keep him safe. Keep Your angels encamped around him to give him hope and strength. Please break this vicious cycle that has our family in the path of destruction. I ask this in Jesus holy name, amen."*

CHAPTER XXVI

Marcus has been served five meals since being abducted. He knows that means he's been there at least three days. Three days naked in the dark. Three days without human contact, except for his feeder twice a day. Three days of constant prayer. Three days of pushups, sit ups, and running in place to keep his mind and body active, and three days of absolute loneliness the kind of which he has never felt before. Marcus prepares himself both mentally and physically for another day of the same routine looking for gaps in the system he can exploit; however, little does he know, help is on the way.

On the other side of the city, Charlie and Mr. Netumba are settling in at Marcus' hotel. Charlie goes into her brother's room, drops her bags and plops down on the bed, as Mr. Netumba enters the room of his fallen warriors. His initial feeling is one of sadness and loss, which is immediately followed by intense anger and revenge. He grabs his phone and makes the call to the waiting navy seals and tells them where he is and to meet him there in 30 minutes. Charlie is sitting on the edge of the bed sobbing when Mr. Netumba burst through the door with a fierce look on his face.

"I'm going to get your brother. Stay here, in this room, until I return with him."

"You better bring him back alive too, Mr. Netumba."

"I'll do my very best."

Mr. Netumba changes into his black fatigues and heads downstairs to meet his new crew. The introductions are made and the team leader turns over command of the team to Mr. Netumba. He pulls out his GPS signal locator and adjusts the frequency for the receiver in Marcus' belt. The signal is traced and the team jumps in the van and speeds off in its direction. The signal is strong around what appears to be an old abandoned prison, and the team circles the building to survey the area. As they are completing their survey of the south entrance of the building, they notice two guards outside the compound entrance trying to blend into the surroundings, seemingly to go unnoticed. Mr. Netumba decides to wait until dark before they breach the compound to take their enemy by surprise. While they wait, he takes the time to prepare his team.

"Okay men, this is a no prisoner mission. Anybody gets in your way, dispose of them quickly and quietly. Here is a picture of the civilian we are here to rescue. Be accurate and careful, I'm not losing any more men on this mission. You die, and I follow you to hell and kill you again myself."

"Yes sir. We won't fail you sir."

As darkness enters its beginning stages, the five man team, plus Mr. Netumba, exit the van and proceed towards their target. Their first objective is to take out the two guards, quietly. This phase takes only a matter of seconds, and because of the speed and accuracy of the team, death comes swiftly for the guards. The team spreads out over the grounds and silently moves in towards the main building following the homing signal. The place appears deserted except for the six remaining guards and Marcus, so the team has no resistance in reaching the main building.

The guards inside are so engrossed in their game of poker that they are totally unaware of the Seal team. As far as the guards knew, no one even knew they were there, so they had no thought of anyone attempting to penetrate the compound. The seal team quickly positions themselves behind several columns approximately 100 yards from the unsuspecting poker players. Using only eye contact, orders are given to each seal, and with the silencers attached to their sub-machine guns, they start to make their move. One of the seals mistakenly kicks a rock and the poker playing guards are alerted that something is afoot.

The guards all reach for their weapons and slowly rise from the table and begin to look around. As they were trained to do at the first sign of trouble, two of the guards back up towards the elevator and push the button to go down. As they search the darkness with their eyes, they were unable to tell where their attackers are, and took a kneeling position to prevent from being standing targets. The other four guards reach to turn over the poker table, when the bell for the elevator sounds and immediately shots begin to pierce the darkness. The front four guards are instantly taken out and the other two dive into the elevator with bullets flying from every direction. As the doors close, one of the guards lies on the floor of the elevator dead and the other is sitting beside him with a bullet in his thigh. He knows that he has very little time to get to his prisoner before his attackers make it downstairs. He limps out of the elevator and makes his way down the hall to Marcus' cell. The guard, now frantic, hears the seal team coming down the stairs. Marcus hears the commotion and backs up into the corner behind the cell door cloaked by the darkness. His captor opens the door and steps into the doorway, and before he can say or do anything, Marcus forcefully kicks the door into the guard's face and then grabs his head and slams it against the wall. Marcus doesn't give him a chance to recover, he grabs the guard's head and places one hand on his chin and the other on the back of his head, and twists it until he hears his neck snap and the guard is lying lifeless on the floor. Marcus grabs his blanket, wraps himself in it, picks up the guard's weapon and retreats back into his cell and takes position in the darkest corner of the room.

Mr. Netumba and the seals finally make it down the four flights of stairs, and as they reach the bottom, they turn on the flashlights attached to their guns to light up the dark corridor with the occasional flickering light. Mr. Netumba raises his hand to stop the team and checks his GPS. He turns in the direction of the signal and notices Marcus' clothes lying on the floor in the corner. Before he lets his team advance, he calls out into the darkness.

"Marcus, Marcus Howard, are you in here?!"

"Who's out there?"

"It's the agent you met at your home. Are you okay?"

"I'm fine, but you need to prove who you are."

"How?"

"How many agents were at my house that day?"

"It was night and there were seven counting me and you were wearing a ring given to you by your father."

"Turn on the light next to the elevator and I'll come out."

Zuri reaches over and turns on the lights. Marcus exits his cell and enters the corridor wrapped in his blanket armed with the dead guard's weapon. Once his eyes adjust to the light, he recognizes Zuri as the agent at his house and lowers his newly acquired weapon.

"About time you got here."

"Better late than never."

"Where are my clothes?"

"Right here. Where is the guy who came down in the elevator?"

"Dead in my cell, I had to kill him."

"Damn Marcus, you're alright!"

"It was either him or me and obviously I have more to live for than he did because he enjoyed being here all day."

"Okay then. Let's get you out of here."

"Can I have my clothes first please?"

"I'm sorry, of course you can. Without these clothes, we wouldn't have known where to find you."

"Where are the guys you had watching me?"

"They're dead."

"I'm sorry to hear that, they were great guys. I didn't really know them, but we had a connection because they were always around."

"They were both great guys. Now, do you know who it was that ordered your abduction? Do you have a name?"

"I know exactly who it was. His name is Zuka Tsimba. He introduced himself to me and said he would take me to the ruling council. When he grabbed me, the first thing he did was take my father's ring, and I want it back."

"Let's get you back to the hotel and cleaned up and then we can talk about that."

"Let me tell you something Mr. . . . ."

"Just call me Zuri."

"Mr. Zuri, all I need is a good meal, a change of clothes and the directions to the ruling council, and I'll take care of the rest."

"Listen Marcus, I know you're ready to go, but there are some things you are unaware of and I need to brief you on all that information."

"Now you listen, Mr. Zuri, a murderer is trying to marry my woman, I was abducted by another mad man, who stole part of my legacy, I was stripped naked and locked in a cell for days, and I had to kill a man with my bare hands to survive; and for what? I'm ready to get to the bottom of this and I mean soon."

"Spoken like a true warrior. Marcus I have the answers you seek. So let's just go back to the hotel, take a shower and we will talk about it all over a good meal. Besides, I have a surprise for you."

"Sure, okay, but you guys go ahead and I'll be right up."

Zuri and his team grab the dead body and head up the elevator. The seal team gathers all the fallen guards in one location. After they drop off Zuri and Marcus, they will come back and make them disappear for good. But for now, Marcus goes back into his cell and kneels down to say a prayer.

"Thank You God for rescuing me from this ordeal. Please forgive me for having to take the life of another man. Thank You for the brave men You sent to rescue me. Bless their lives and the lives of their families. Please find forgiveness for those who lost their lives here today because of me. I pray that You bless the souls of the two fallen warriors who were my protectors and give them peace. Thank You for strengthening me and giving me all I needed to endure. Make me wise enough to discern the meaning of all of this and please continue to guide my steps along the way. My life belongs to You, Your will is my will, You lead and I will follow. Please keep my beloved Zephora safe and help me to return home to her safely. In Jesus name I pray, amen.

CHAPTER XXVII

On the ride back to the hotel, Marcus said nothing. He just stared out of the window biting his bottom lip as he replayed his ordeal in his mind. All he could think about was getting to the bottom of this madness and getting back to his beloved Zephora. He looks down at his hands, they still had blood on them from smashing the soldiers head against the wall, but they were steady. He didn't like what he did, but it was what he had to do to keep his promise; and now he is ready to finish it and go home.

Zuri sits next to Marcus watching him as they ride. He could see the wheels spinning inside Marcus' head. He smiles and thinks to himself "he's ready" as he watches Marcus sort out the details in his mind. Zuri, presumed dead, has worked feverishly behind the scenes and stayed away from his wife and daughter for a very long time in preparation for what is to come next. He turns away from Marcus and like Marcus, looks down at his normally steady hands. Today, at this moment, they are shaking. He clasps them together, presses them against his forehead, and closes his eyes. For the first time in years, Zuri is actually nervous about making the next move. A move that can right an eternal wrong, or destroy the lives of those he swore to protect and loves so dearly.

Upon arriving at the hotel, Marcus, who is still silent, jumps out of the van and heads straight for his room. He opens the door and there sitting on the bed watching television, is Charlie. She jumps up and exclaims "Marcus, you're okay." She starts towards him for a hug, notices he is covered in dirt and blood, and stops dead in her tracks with her mouth wide open in dismay.

"Charlie what in the hell are you doing here?"

The two stand there staring at one another. Charlie is scared to move forward and Marcus is excited and pissed at the same time. His mind is racing. Why is his sister here? Now her life is in danger too. Mr. Zuri has a lot of explaining to do and he better have a damn good explanation.

Zuri, who has been downstairs instructing his team on where to dispose of the bodies, comes back into the hotel and, walks in the door of Marcus' room minutes later. As he closes the door and turns, Marcus clocks him, pushes him against the door, and places his forearm against his throat.

"Why did you bring my sister here? Why are you putting her life in danger?"

Zuri is caught totally off guard by Marcus' quick advances. He is both shocked and thrilled. Marcus is displaying the kind of temperament that Zuri needs to see from him. As encouraged as he is, right now, he needs air and needs to give Marcus an answer.

"Marcus I can explain!"

"I hope so cause I'm about ready to tear you apart for endangering my sister's life."

Charlie grabs Marcus and pulls him off of Zuri. Zuri leans over and puts his hand on his throat as he tries to catch his breath. He is impressed that after being locked up for days, Marcus is so strong.

"Please Marcus," Zuri says, as he gathers himself enough to stand upright.

"Please take a shower and meet us downstairs in 30 minutes. I will explain everything to you then. There's a lot you don't know."

"Okay Mr. Zuri."

"Just Zuri, please."

"Okay Zuri, I will do just that. But when I come downstairs, I will be expecting to hear the truth and only the truth. I will not interrupt you but give you ample opportunity to make sense of all of this to me."

"Thank you, that's all I ask."

Zuri motions to Charlie to come with him and they leave the room. He knows Marcus needs time alone right now to compose himself; however he is pleasantly surprised at how well Marcus is holding up considering all he has been through.

Now alone, Marcus locks the door and then turns on the water in the shower. As he strips down, he stares at himself in the mirror and doesn't recognize the person staring back. Maybe he is too dirty and bloody to recognize himself; whatever the case, for the first time in a long while he didn't know who he was. He is glad Zephora couldn't see him like this, but also wishes she was there.

Marcus steps into the shower and immediately the water begins to rinse away the dirt and blood of the last few days; and with them, tears roll down his face; tears that he is finally able to shed. He stands there and lets the water rush over his body for several minutes before he grabs the soap and wash cloth and begins to scrub himself vigorously as if to scrub away the memory of the last week and watch it spiral down the drain with the dirt, blood and tears. As the water rinses away the remaining filth and soap from his body, Marcus holds his face directly in front of the rushing water and lets the hot water cleanse his pores, and while doing so, hears the still voice of the Lord say, *"You are not alone, I am still with you."* Marcus drops his head and whispers, "Thank you."

Fresh out of the shower, Marcus wipes the moisture from the mirror and again stares at himself as he dries off. This time he sees a familiar face, smiles and says "hello you." Now clean, Marcus takes the time to shave his head and trim his beard, and just like that, he is back to himself but with a few improvements: wiser, smarter, stronger, more patient and determined than ever. Marcus finishes up in the bathroom and commences to pull out his favorite suit, shirt, and tie and hangs them over the door. He then sits on the edge of the bed to lotion his legs and feet. Once done, and still with the towel wrapped around his waist, Marcus lies back on the bed and gives a big sigh of relief.

Meanwhile, in the adjacent room, Zuri and Charlie prepare to go downstairs for dinner. It is late but the two are starving.

"Come on Charlie let's grab a bite before they close the kitchen."

"Shouldn't we wait for Marcus?"

"Unless I miss my guess, your brother is crashed out across the bed. He's been through a lot and definitely needs the rest."

"Then why did you tell him we would meet him?"

"With all that adrenaline coursing through his veins, I had to calm him down some way."

"You're right, lead the way."

As Charlie and Zuri enjoy a meal and conversation, Marcus lay passed out across the bed exhausted from his ordeal. It is the first peaceful rest he has had in a while. The adrenaline was like a massive sugar rush and once he calmed down he crashed. After all he has been through he needed it; not to mention, the challenges still ahead of him. Rest well Marcus, for tomorrow will bring its own tests for you.

CHAPTER XXVIII

It's morning and Marcus rolls over on his bed and pulls the comforter over his head. His eye catches a glimpse of light as the comforter is pulled across his face. It is then he realizes that he has slept the night away and missed his meeting with Zuri. For a moment he feels panicked, but in true Marcus form he gathers himself understanding that whatever he missed obviously had to wait, especially since no one came to wake him up. Marcus is still draped in his towel from his shower last night and his clothes are hanging just where he left them. Now fully awake, he gets on his knees and takes the time to thank God for a peaceful nights rest, waking him up and giving him another opportunity to be better than he was the day before. He prays for strength, courage and wisdom, and says a prayer for his beloved Zephora. He says prayers for their families, friends and even their enemies. He asks for guidance and the boldness to say and do what must be done. He ends his prayers by saying "In Jesus holy name, Amen." With his morning prayer done, Marcus heads to the bathroom to wash his face, brush his teeth and mentally prepare his self for the day.

Charlie and Zuri have been up for a while now so they are dressed and ready to go. On their way downstairs, Zuri knocks on Marcus' door and yells "breakfast downstairs in fifteen minutes Marcus!" With his clothes already ironed and ready, Marcus, being anxious to have his conversation with Zuri, actually makes it downstairs in ten minutes only to find Zuri and Charlie already on their first cup of coffee. As he approaches the table, Charlie jumps up to greet him with the big hug and kiss on the cheek that she was reluctant to give him last night. Zuri stands up to shake Marcus' hand and acknowledges how much better Marcus looks this morning. Marcus takes the time to express his profound gratitude to Zuri for rescuing him. The three sit down and the waiter comes over and pours Marcus a cup of coffee and refills the cups of Charlie and Zuri. Marcus is ready to get some answers; however, he decides to show patience and wait for Zuri to speak first. After taking a few sips of her coffee, Charlie looks up and smiles at her little brother.

"Marcus you look fabulous; a far cry from the way you looked last night."

"Why thank you dear sister. I...," Marcus replies. But before he could get another word out, she interrupts him mid-sentence.

"I know you're wondering why I'm here, and I assure you I have a good reason."

"I hope so, because I'm sure you realize by now this place is extremely dangerous."

"Yeah, but Zuri has taken really good care of me during our travels together."

"Yeah, I bet he has," Marcus says sharply and cuts his eyes over at Zuri who sets down his cup and returns the glare by tilting his head to the side, pursing his lips and connecting his eyes with Marcus'.

"Not like that dummy," Charlie retorts, "he has been the perfect gentleman and taken me places and shown me things and helped me find out things about our family that are pretty deep."

"And where exactly did he take you and what did you find out?" The two of them are locked in conversation as if Zuri wasn't sitting there at all.

"He took me to the Bahamas and while there, I met one of our relatives that we had no idea about."

"The Bahamas, really, you know I do some business there with a company named Babwean Imports? The owner's name is Madam Zigumba."

This is the last thing Charlie had expected her brother to say. How is it that he has been doing business with Madam Zigumba and never told her about this distance relative?

"Marcus you know her and you never told me about her?

"Why should I? I do business with a lot of people most of whom you don't know, nor did I think you ever cared to know."

"Don't you know who she is?"

"Yeah, a nice old lady who happens to import and export goods like I do. What's the big deal?"

"Marcus, she's our great aunt!"

"What are you talking about?"

"Before our father…"

"Your father," Marcus interrupts.

"Anyway, before he went home he gave me some papers with an address on them that is the location of Babwean Imports and he told me to give them to the owner. It turns out that she is also the same person that Zuri was taking me to the

Bahamas to see. And once we sat down and talked, she gave me a briefcase filled with papers about our family heritage. You, my dear brother, are next in line to be king of this country and we are rich!"

Marcus is calm. He doesn't react; he just sits there drinking his coffee. His mind is digesting the information while trying to make sense out of what is going on. While he sits there contemplating, Charlie reaches down, picks up the briefcase and sets it on the chair next to Marcus. Marcus begins to replay events in his mind: the ring his father gave him, the reaction of Zuka when he saw the ring and his kidnapping because of the ring. It is a lot to process all at once, and he needs more answers.

"Okay Zuri, it's time you tell me what is going on here."

Zuri takes another sip of coffee, slowly sets the cup on the table, and begins to speak. "Marcus all I ask is that you do me a favor and please don't interrupt or ask any questions until I'm finished."

"Fair enough, now let's have it."

Zuri starts out by telling Marcus that he is Zephora's father. Marcus doesn't even blink; he just continues to listen without saying a word. Zuri continues to explain how their two families were part of the ruling nobles from centuries ago. The story was beginning to sound like the one Kwazan told him in the hospital; except in the version Zuri is telling him now, Marcus' ancestors were a part of this council. Zuri keeps talking and explains how the betrayal and greed of Kwazan and Zuka's families got Marcus' family exiled and because Zuri's ancestors overheard this betrayal, they were to be assassinated. He explains how they escaped and came to be in America. He tells Marcus that it was Kwazan's father who killed Zephora's grandfather and thought he had killed Zuri too. To protect his family, it was best they thought he was dead. Kwazan's father didn't know about Zephora at the time and Zuri knew his wife would know what to do if he didn't come home. That is when he became a CIA operative. The job gave him the opportunity to keep tabs on his family and seek out leads on the exiled family of the council. And it wasn't until he came across someone, that someone being Charlie, looking into the Howard family ancestry that he found the missing link he was looking for. He then directs Marcus' attention to the birthmark that both he and Charlie share; a birthmark that all their ancestors share.

221

"Marcus, they kidnapped you because you had on the ring of the true ruling family for this century. You are the rightful heir to lead the council for the next hundred years not Kwazan."

While Zuri was telling his story, they all ordered their breakfast. Though Zuri was finished talking, Marcus didn't say a word. Their breakfast arrives and Marcus still has said nothing. Once all the plates are on the table, Marcus prays over the food and begins to eat without saying another word. Charlie and Zuri are puzzled by Marcus' reaction or lack thereof. So they decide to eat as well and everyone was totally silent except for the occasional smacking and clinking of forks on the plates. Marcus finishes his breakfast first. He drinks down a glass of orange juice and motions to the waiter for another cup of coffee. He sips his coffee and allows Zuri and Charlie to finish their breakfast before he says a word.

"Now that we have all finished breakfast, let me see if I got this straight. You are Zephora's father whom she thinks is dead; she is the rightful queen to be and I am the rightful king to be of this ruling council in this land that is filled with starving people and a dysfunctional president; and you have known this the whole time and just chose not to tell anyone?"

"That's right."

"Now Kwazan and his cohorts didn't know about me being heir until Zuka just happen to see me with the ring on?

"Yes, and Marcus, I didn't tell you because I needed to have the ancestral historical data to prove my claim before I said anything. Had I said anything anytime sooner, you would probably be dead already. This country may look poor; however, this is not the truth. The riches are being hoarded by those in power and you and my daughter have a chance to change that. What I have done and what I do is for my family and for my people, your people, our people."

"Okay Zuri, so what's our next move?"

Charlie is baffled by her brother's cool demeanor. She knows he is usually as cool as a cucumber, but after all that information all he wants to know is "what's our next move?" She can't help but chime in. "Marcus you are taking this all very well."

"Charlie, in the last six weeks I've gone from the altar to Africa. I've been followed, had men attack me in my home, been kidnapped and to top it all off, I had to kill a man with my bare hands. Not to mention that there is a murdering mad man trying to marry my fiancé. I am all out of the shocked and dismayed reaction. I just want to put an end to all of this and get home. So, like I said, Zuri, what is our next move?"

"Marcus, last night I had my team locate Zuka Tsimba and retrieve your ring, and here it is." Marcus takes the ring and nods to gesture thank you to prevent from interrupting Zuri. "I also had them detain him. While they did their job, I got to work and made some phone calls to get in touch with the rest of the council. Once I made contact, I met with them and presented them with copies of the information Charlie and I received from Madam Zigumba. I further let them know about you and your sister, and about the birthmark you both possess on your legs that are consistent with your family history. Reluctantly they heard my plea; and after I explained to them how Zuka Tsimba kidnapped you, they were willing to review my evidence. They have requested that I get a blood sample from you to verify you are indeed from this region and of the royal council. Supposedly, they have DNA of all the original families of the council since it was a blood treaty and the original eight knives were preserved. So if you would allow me to get a sample from you, I will get it processed today and tomorrow we will have the results and meet with the council."

"Well, haven't you been busy? First, thank you for getting my ring back, and second, what is going to happen to Zuka? But before you answer that question, tell me how can this supposed ruling council with all its wealth allow this country to be in such turmoil? How can they sit back and allow the so called president of this country to get away with the crimes he has and still is committing? What kind of a council are they, and why should I want to be a part of any of this?"

"Apparently, the council has been run by Zuka and Kwazan. Their fathers took control of the council years ago after the mysterious deaths of some council members' children. Both Zuka and Kwazan have ties to the president and keep him funded. The corruption here is intense and once we can get you and my daughter married and in charge, you will have the power to start changing things in this entire region. You have seen the pain, anguish and the suffering in the faces of the people; don't you want to be a part of saving them and bringing this country back to greatness?"

The three finish their breakfast and go back upstairs where Zuri gets a sample of blood from Marcus. While Zuri is out getting the sample processed, Marcus and Charlie take the time to catch up and swap stories and adventures. The two of them never could have imagined they would be in this position or even in Africa for that matter. Charlie takes the time to tell Marcus how she got mixed up with Zuri and that she didn't know who he was for a long time; she just knew that he was trying to help.

Marcus tells her of his ordeal and of the beautiful country he explored since he has been here. He shares how much he misses Zephora and prays she is okay. He has not been in contact with her in so long, but he doesn't want to call her until he knows exactly what is going to happen here. Marcus and Charlie share tears, laughs and hugs. The duo have placed a lot of trust in Zuri, and so far he has not let either of them down.

As the day passes on, the new royal siblings have talked as if they had not seen one another for years. They talked over lunch which they had in Marcus' room and talked more after that. Right before dinner, Zuri arrives at the hotel with the lab results in hand. The three have dinner and Zuri lets them know that they are scheduled to meet the council in the morning at 9:00 am at the U.S. Embassy. Zuri also lets Marcus know that his team will be bringing Zuka as well. With all the details in place, Marcus takes a moment to change the subject.

"So Zuri, how are you going to explain to Zephora and Saphera why you are alive and why you haven't contacted them?"

"Marcus, a long time ago I had to make a decision to leave my family in order to protect them. I became a federal agent in order to be able to keep my eye on them. I have missed them both terribly and cannot wait to hold them both again. I love my wife and daughter more than anyone in this world, especially my daughter. No one could love her more."

"I beg to differ. I assure you I love her far more than you."

"Different kind of love son, but I get the point. Hopefully all this will be resolved tomorrow and I can get you back to her. By the way, my guys tell me she is doing fine. She and her mother are planning the wedding as requested by Kwazan and the wedding is to take place in a day."

"What!! Are we going to make it back in time to stop it?"

"The council received the same results I did so in the morning we should be able to prove the validity of our claim, have you sworn in as the new head of the council, sign a few official papers, go to the bank to give you access to your inheritance, then get on a plane back home."

"Good because I am ready to get home and get back to my life and my wife."

"Marcus, your wife will be there, but your life is never going to be the same again. You must return here to set things right."

"Oh, right."

The evening comes to a close and the three return to their rooms to get some more well needed rest. Marcus finds it hard to sleep thinking about the challenge before him. He is expected to turn around a country and save his beloved from a maniac. Life was much simpler before he found all this out. He ran his business and loved his woman. As of tomorrow he will be the head of the ruling council in a country bent on destroying itself, and let's not forget, he will also be extremely wealthy. It's a big change for a poor boy from the south. Before he climbs into bed, Marcus takes the time to pray.

Father, thank you for the opportunities you have placed before me. Grant me the wisdom to lead in a way worthy of Your approval. Protect these people Father, and continue to take care of their needs. Bless this council with Your forgiveness for their actions or lack of actions. Bless them with grace and mercy. Fill the dark places in their hearts with Your cleansing light. I ask for Your favor at this meeting tomorrow and in everything I do. Please continue to protect Zephora and her mother and grant them peace of mind and comfort. I thank You for Zuri and pray that You continue to bless his life and to reunite him with his family. I ask these things in Jesus Holy name, Amen.

CHAPTER XXIX

It's 6:00 a.m., and Marcus is already downstairs and having a cup of coffee. He is dressed to impress and ready to go. He knows the meeting isn't for another three hours; however, he is taking the time to prepare his mind, body and spirit. He is used to getting up early and takes this time to use the hotel computer to send an email to Angelo. He had not spoken to him since he left and he knows if he lets Angelo know he is alive that Angelo will somehow get that information to Zephora. He sits in front of the computer wondering exactly what to say to his impetuous friend to keep him calm and assured of his well-being.

> *Hello Angelo. How is the business doing? I am doing fine and have loads to tell you. Charlie is over here with me and she is fine too. We are expecting to be back in a couple of days. Find a way to let Zephora know I am fine and that's all. Thanks for handling business for me partner, can't wait to get home, take care and I will see you guys soon. Oh yeah, how are things going with Veronica? Can't wait for the update.*

Hopefully Angelo will only do what he asked and nothing more. You never know with Angelo. Marcus takes the time to do some research on the country and its state of affairs; nothing like being prepared before a big meeting.

It's 7:00 a.m., and Zuri and Charlie join Marcus in the café for breakfast. Few words are spoken except for the normal pleasantries. It seems that everyone is in deep thought this morning and not in the mood to talk. They barely look up at one another while they devour their breakfast. Marcus decides he needs to lighten up the mood a little, so he decides to tell a joke.

"Okay, you guys are a buzz kill so I got a joke for you to lighten the mood. What's the best way to start your day?"

Charlie responds, "What is the best way to start your day?"

"Sunny side up," shouts Marcus.

Both Charlie and Zuri look up and barely crack a smile. Marcus retorts, "I tried," and continues eating. Zuri finishes his breakfast first and takes the opportunity to brief Marcus.

"Marcus, these guys are not going to like you much at first. They have been betrayed and dishonored and are in no mood to play games. They know that you are the rightful heir;

however, to them you are an outsider. What you say will determine the type of relationship you will have with them."

"Thank you Zuri. I'm ready, I have been up for a while getting prepared for this meeting and I think I'm ready; but if you have any advice; I would love to hear it."

"My only advice for you is not to appear scared or weak. They will pick up on it right away and refuse to follow you."

"Thank you, I will keep that in mind."

It's 8:45 a.m., and Marcus, Charlie, and Zuri arrive at the embassy. They are escorted into the embassy by armed guard and taken to a large conference room. Sitting at the table are the six members of the council and in the corner, handcuffed and guarded, is Zuka. Kwazan would have rounded out the members to eight, but since he is in the U.S. trying to pull off his coo and his collaborator caught, he has no idea of this meeting. Charlie and Zuri take seats on the side of the conference table opposite the council members, and Marcus pulls out the chair at the head of the table and remains standing. He glances over at Zuka who catches his eye and then lowers his head. Marcus then turns his attention to the other council members and addresses them.

"My fellow council members my name is Marcus Howard, and I am a direct descendant of the Sakara family, one of the original members of this tribal council. By Tribal Law, I take control of this council as it is my birthright. Anyone who opposes this action should stand and be acknowledged."

All of the council members have reviewed all the data and are agreement that Marcus' claim is legit, so none of them stand. Zuka, who is in the corner, tries to rise to his feet, but is pushed back down on his chair by the guard next to him.

"I further decree that Zuri Netumba receive his seat on this tribal council, as he is a direct descendant of one of this tribal council's original members as well. Arrangements are to be made to imprison Zuka for the rest of his life for the attempt on my life and to remove his family name from this council; and, when I return to the U.S., I will have Kwazan detained and expedited back here for the same punishment. It will take me sometime to become fully abreast of all the information about my country and why it is suffering so, but to help me in this transition, I appoint Mr. Netumba as my official liaison on internal affairs. I am totally appalled at the condition of my people and vow to work with you gentlemen to bring our country to the greatness it rightfully deserves. Together we can forge a new era for our people, which to my understanding, was the purpose of this council in the first place."

The members of the council, Zuri and Charlie all stand and clap in recognition of Marcus' speech. As they all sit back down, one member remains standing and addresses Marcus.

"Mr. Howard, my name is Mashama Bengono and I speak for the members of this council before you. We first apologize for the injustice that your family and Mr. Netumba's family suffered by the hands of the unscrupulous members of this council, past and present. We reviewed all the data provided by Mr. Netumba and we are honored to have you here and pledge our allegiance to you for the duration of your reign and the reign of your family for the next 100 years, and your family as members of this tribal council until the end of time. We have been made aware of the situation with Kwazan in the U.S. and have prepared the royal jet for your departure. We have also set up accounts for you and Mr. Netumba that transfer the holdings of Zuka and Kwazan to you. All we need is your signature on these official bank forms."

"Thank you Mr. Bengono; however, before I leave let's get a few things straight. First, the past and present so called members who betrayed this council and our families were and are criminals of this country and it should be documented that way for all time. Second, before I return, I fully expect the corrupt so called president of this country be removed from office and a fair election to be held. This council has failed to protect the people from oppression and it is time we effectively do our patriotic duty. There is enough blame to go around; however, I choose not to blame but empower. Mr. Netumba and I have had these proceedings recorded, typed and printed. Our assistant has placed in front of you the outcome of this meeting and the acknowledgement of your acceptance of me as the new ruling council member. It requires all of our signatures to make this official. This council has worked in secret for centuries steering this country down a path of destruction and now it is time the destruction ends and a new direction be forged that changes the lives of its entire people. I am looking forward to working together with all of you to help create the political and societal success of The Great Zimbabwe and its sister society Mapungubwe here in Malawi, in this century and in our lifetime."

With the signing of the official documents behind him, Marcus takes the time to talk to every member of the tribal council and extend his hand to them and introduce them to Charlie. Zuka is taken away without a word or even a second look from Marcus. Zuri motions to Marcus and Charlie that it is time to leave and the three say their goodbyes and head to the bank, back to the hotel and then to the private airstrip where the royal jet is waiting. While in route to the hotel, Zuri takes the time to talk to Marcus about the way he handled the council members at the meeting.

"Marcus, I am so very proud of you son. You handled yourself with control and poise. You spoke only on what was important at the time and nothing more. It was outstanding and you established yourself as a competent leader in their eyes. Your days of financial struggle are over; but your days of leadership struggles have just begun. One thing you must remember about the tribal council is that it works behind the scene to influence the direction of the country and you must be able to continue in this tradition. However, that was a moment of great pride for me and I am honored to have you as my leader and my son-in-law."

"Thank you Zuri, but it is me who is honored to know you and serve you. I hope to be able to live up to the standards you have set for me."

"The standards I have for you are no more or less than the standards you have already set for yourself and display in your life on a daily basis."

Charlie, who has been silent this entire time, interrupts to add in her two cents worth.

"Okay you two, enough with honoring one another. Are we leaving this place or what? I for one am ready to get home and sleep in my own bed. All this traveling is great, but there is no place like home. And what about Zephora; are you guys going to call her and let her know what is going on? You know she is worried sick about Marcus and is probably going crazy by now."

"First my darling sister, yes, we are out of here. Our bags have already been packed and are being transported to the plane, and after we check out, we are headed directly to the airstrip. And as for my precious Zephora, I have decided not to tell her anything yet. We will get back just in time to stop the wedding; and since I am already dressed to impress, I think turnabout is fair play, except this time, the wedding will go on with me as the groom."

"Marcus, what do you do, come up with these plans days in advance? You are so crazy, and I hope Zephora slaps your face for putting her through all this mess."

Zuri chimes in, "I don't know Marcus I tend to agree with Charlie on this one. You should call Zephora and let her know."

"What about you Zuri? How are you going to explain all this to Zephora and Saphera? I would think you would side with me on this one. Let's just be prepared to explain it after I officially become your son-in-law."

"Good point Marcus. Oh well Charlie, you have been overruled."

Charlie looks at them with disgust and turns her head away to look out the window. The three are all ready to get back home and each take the time to lay theirs head back and reflect on their individual journeys. Zuri's journey started so many years ago with having to leave his family to keep them alive and not being able to watch his daughter grow up or be a part of her life. He will now have the chance to really get to know her and reunite with his beloved Saphera after all this time. Marcus' journey started when Kwazan interrupted his wedding. He can't wait to get back to his beloved Zephora. He has missed her tremendously and is anxious to look into her beautiful brown eyes and tell her how much he loves her once again. He also has gained a good friend in Zuri, and he finally knows where his roots began. Charlie's journey began when she first decided to look up their ancestral history. Had she not took the time to be thorough in her search, she might have never got to meet her great aunt, see the Bahamas, or even go to Africa.

It's 12:00 p.m. Malawi time, and Marcus, Zuri, and Charlie are aboard the private jet bound for the U.S. The flight is a long one, thirteen hours, but only six real time hours because of the time difference, and it will be a good opportunity to get some sleep before the next phase of their journey together. The skies are clear as the plane flies over beautiful Africa and Marcus turns to look out of the window and say his goodbyes to the continent that tried to claim his life but ended up rewarding him greatly for his courage and integrity. He can't wait to get home and deal Kwazan the final blow, reclaim his bride and start their new life together.

CHAPTER XXX

In eight hours Zephora is going to marry a man who is the enemy of her husband, the poisoner of her mother, and a man she can't bear to look at; and she must do this to save the life of the one man she truly loves. The cruelty of this man has caused him to instruct Zephora to set up the wedding at the same church, with the same pastor, the same guest list and the same time. Zephora is frantic, she has not heard from Marcus and her nerves are starting to get the best of her.

Saphera walks in the room to find her daughter crying her eyes out and ruining her makeup. "Zephora," she screams, "you have got to pull yourself together we cannot keep redoing your makeup!"

"Is that all you can think about, my makeup? My supposed to be husband is missing, and I hate my going to be husband. I don't care how my makeup looks, my life is over."

"Your life is not over my dear, you are about to become a queen and part of the most powerful couple in an African country; and, extremely wealthy I might add. You will be able to do and go wherever you want; that includes seeing Marcus."

"Money, power and infidelity; is that all you think about? Is that what you want my life to be about? I can't believe you sometimes, there's more to my life, more to me, than that. I have been a trusting child of God most of life and I refuse to believe that the God I serve will allow things to work out this way for me."

"Well my darling if that is what you believe, stop crying and get ready and let's see what happens. I know this is tough, but we can do it, together. I will be there with you every step of the way."

Seven hours to go and mother and daughter are now calm and getting prepared to walk Zephora down the aisle again. Veronica comes in the room and Zephora begins to cry all over again as she gets up to give her best friend a hug.

"My God Veronica, I just got her to stop crying and now you have ruined her makeup again. You're doing it this time, I'm done," shouts Saphera.

"What's her deal Zephora, you would think she's the one marrying a murdering tyrant," exclaims Veronica.

"I think this is her way of dealing with all of this; acting like she doesn't care and the only thing that matters is money and power."

"I don't know girl, sounds like she's losing her mind to me. Now let's get you ready to go."

"Thanks Veronica; I'm glad you're here because this is some fraganagal bull."

The two of them share a long embrace and get busy getting Zephora ready for the wedding no woman dreams of ever having. In the midst of their preparations, Zephora receives a text from Angelo that simply states that Marcus is alive and well and she need not worry about him. She texts him back to see if he would be at the wedding. Angelo tells her that he will be there but he didn't know where Marcus was or if he would make it. Veronica is pleased that Zephora heard from Angelo. She and Angelo have been seeing one another the entire time Marcus has been away and their new relationship has promise. This information gives Zephora something to smile about.

Knowing that Marcus is okay is great news; however, not knowing if she would ever see him again negated that bit of good news and brought a bit of sorrow over her already burdened heart. She doesn't know how much more she can bear. Now she receives another text, this one from Kwazan stating he will see her at the church and can barely contain himself. She had wondered how much more; and there it came, just a little more and she takes it and refuses to cry anymore. If this is what she has to bare in order to save the life of the man she loves, she will be as brave as he must be for not being able to be with her. They may physically be apart, but their spirits will always be together. She just only wishes she could talk to him. He has always been the rock that kept her grounded in times of trouble and anguish. Now, she must do it from the memory of him in her heart.

It's 2:15 p.m., and the wedding is about six hours away.

Meanwhile, its 6:00 p.m., Marcus' plane has landed and the threesome has made it in record time. Marcus instructs the limo driver to take them by his house before going to the church so he can change into his tux, and then calls Angelo and requests he meet them there as well.

"Marcus," expresses Zuri, "don't you think we're cutting this just a little bit close?"

"No, when I see my bride, I want her to see me ready to marry her at that moment just the way I am supposed to be. What we should be concerning ourselves with is our plan upon our arrival."

Zuri responds with his plan of conquest. "I suggest we wait in the foyer of the church where we cannot be seen but we can hear everything. I will dispatch a team of my men to guard the exits of the church and to quietly take out any of Kwazan's men who will undoubtedly warn him of our arrival. Once we hear the preacher ask the "just cause" question, we will open the doors and show ourselves and take Kwazan by surprise."

Marcus likes the plan and now with his tux on is ready to go. Though he seems calm, his heart is racing as it has been close to sixty days since he last saw his love or even talked to her; not to mention, this will also be his wedding day. He is extremely excited and a little scared as well as nervous. His life has changed dramatically in two months, and he is surely wiser than he was before. He has learned to be more patient, learned the value of life and not to take time for granted for none is promised to anyone. He must not only be ready to be a husband but also the leader of a corporation and a country. He is also wealthier than he ever thought possible and now also has a stronger sense of family and devotion to that family. With his queen by his side, he knows he can accomplish anything he desires. Her love and her strength strengthen him and fill him with a sense of purpose that cannot be denied.

It's 7:00 p.m. and the people have begun to fill the church in anticipation of the impending nuptials. Kwazan has arrived with his men and sits in the church office with the minister. Pastor Chappell poses a question to the would be leader as he does with each and every man who sits in his office awaiting his turn to be wed.

"Young man, have you reconciled in your heart any issues that would cause you distress in this marriage; have you prayed and asked God to grant you the wisdom needed to be a husband; have you emotionally and physically parted from any woman that may cause issues in your marriage; do you understand the level of commitment, integrity and perseverance needed for a successful marriage; do you understand the seven applications of marriage that ground and guide a successful marriage; and finally, have you declared in your heart to be faithful forever to your bride to be?"

"None of what you say matters to me. This is a matter of my right by order of Tribal Law in accordance with the ruling council of my people. The woman that awaits me is but the culmination of my destiny and the prize and proof of my achievement and nothing more."

"May God have mercy upon your soul my son; for you have not spoken of love in any of what you have said and thus have doomed Zephora to a life of misery."

"Preacher, you are correct, but you will be marrying us just the same."

It's 7:45 p.m. and the church is now filled with the guest for this frightful occasion. Zephora, Saphera and Veronica have now arrived and are taking their places in the church foyer. Zephora begins to wonder if this is what life has come to? Did my faithful walk lead me here to take the hand of a violent and murdering man who would have the love of my life killed? Sadness has overtaken her as she pulls the veil over her face. The doors to the sanctuary open and Veronica begins her walk down the aisle in a slow and deliberate way walking beside one of Kwazan's henchmen. As they reach the end of their walk, they take their places and await the signal from Pastor Chappell for the entrance of the bride.

It's 8:00 p.m. and Pastor Chappell says "all rise," and the people rise and turn to face the bride. It has been a long time since a bride has looked this beautiful. Her dress slopes off her shoulders and accents every curve of her body. It is so white that Zephora seems to glow as she takes each step. The dress flows to the floor with a three foot train that follows.

It is 8:05 p.m. and Zephora with her mother beside her has reached the front of the church. "Who gives this woman away to wed this man?" "I, her mother, do give her away to wed this man." Saphera raises Zephora's veil, kisses her on the cheek and takes her seat with tears in her eyes.

Zephora takes a step up and faces Kwazan and closes her eyes. She remembers standing here two months ago and being overjoyed to do so. She remembers standing here facing the man of her dreams ready to commit her life to him and her eyes being filled with enormous tears of joy. Now she stands here with only contempt in her heart for the man she is facing, the man she cannot bare to look at, which is why her eyes are closed so tightly they could not be pried apart.

Pastor Chappell begins, "Marriage is an institution that should not be entered into lightly." Unknown to everyone in the sanctuary, Charlie, Angelo, Zuri and Marcus are on the other side of the doors of the sanctuary awaiting the magic words that would enable them to crash this sad occasion.

Pastor Chappell continues. "The union of a man and a woman is the most important relationship two can enter into, besides the relationship each and every individual should have with themselves and with God Almighty. It is not just a promise between the two of them which they enter into, but also a promise which they make separately and together with God as well. And it is for that very reason; we are having this ceremony today in front of God and in front of all you witnesses. Now, with that being said, and before I go any further, I ask all here in attendance today, if you know of any just cause why these two people should not be joined as one here today to speak now or forever hold your peace."

FINAL CHAPTER

It's 8:20 p.m., and once again, as it was two months ago, the sanctuary falls so quiet you can hear a pin drop. Although many in attendance knew this marriage should not be, out of fear none will rise. Kwazan stands there smiling and full of himself because he knows no one will dare challenge him. Zephora stands in front of him with her eyes still clinched shut and praying, *"Please God save me from this menace to society. Please God do not have me marry this man I cannot stand to look at, let alone let him touch me. Please, in the name of Jesus, save me from a life of misery."* At that moment, the doors of the sanctuary fly open and a deep loud voice shouts "I OBJECT TO THIS WEDDING!" Every person in the church turns toward the rear of the church and see....no one. It's 8:24 p.m. and Charlie begins to walk down the center of the aisle, she is followed by Angelo and Zuri walking side by side, and they are followed by Marcus, who is dressed in an ivory six button single breasted tuxedo with a black vest, white shirt adorned with a large black jewel in place of a bowtie.

Zephora begins to smile and praise God with earnestness, and Kwazan turns and begins to unbutton his tux. Saphera, upon seeing her supposedly dead husband shouts "OH MY GOD," and sits back in her seat to keep from fainting.

Marcus graciously walks down the aisle and proudly declares "By Tribal Law, and because Zephora Sherman, the woman I love, the woman who was made just for me, is promised to me!" Zuri unbuttons his coat and reaches for his weapon to arrest Kwazan. Kwazan starts backing up and looking for his men who never arrive because they have been detained. Zephora screams "MARCUS YOU MADE IT!" and runs towards Marcus, being careful not to trip over the train of her dress. Marcus replies "Wouldn't have missed it for the world," as he smoothly steps towards Zephora.

In anger and utter disbelief, Kwazan pulls out a 9mm hand gun and shouts "IF I CANNOT HAVE HER, THEN NO ONE WILL HAVE HER!" Simultaneously, Zuri and Marcus shout "NO," and both of them leap to position themselves between Zephora and Kwazan who discharges two shots from his weapon. As Zuri lunges in front of his daughter, the daughter he hasn't been near all of her life, he instinctively, as he was trained to do, draws his gun and in mid-air fires three shots striking Kwazan center mass in his chest before he and Marcus both hit the floor after successfully diving in front of Zephora, protecting her from Kwazan's discharged bullets.

Screams ring out throughout the sanctuary as the people rush toward the exits fearing for their lives. Within minutes, the church is empty except for the families and friends of the bride and groom. It's 8:30 p.m. Saphera is screaming in her seat, Charlie is kneeling beside her, attempting to calm her down, and Zephora is standing in the same spot she was in when the shooting began and has not moved, she's in shock. After hearing the shots fired and seeing the people rush out, Zuri's men charge in to find Kwazan, Zuri and Marcus all down.

It's 8:35 p.m., and Kwazan has been declared dead by Zuri's men. Zephora and Saphera rush to the side of their respective men, kneeling beside them and placing their heads in their laps. Charlie, Saphera and Zephora are now crowding around Zuri and Marcus who are both unconscious on the floor covered in blood. They are unsure if one or both of them have been struck by the bullets. Angelo shouts "WE NEED A DOCTOR IN HERE, SOMEBODY GET US AN AMBULANCE. HURRY WE NEED A DOCTOR NOW!

"Zephora honey, this is your father lying here with Marcus, I told you I saw him, I told you he was alive," Saphera relents.

Zephora responds, "My who, my what; I thought he was dead, you told me he was dead. Where's the ambulance, they need to hurry, neither of them is moving and I can't tell where or who the blood is coming from."

Angelo attempts to get the ladies to move aside so he can try to tend to Marcus and Zuri; however, Zephora and Saphera refuse to leave the side of their respective men but Charlie, though hysterical, begins to slowly move back as requested by Angelo.

Finally, the ambulance arrives and the paramedics ask the ladies to step back so they may start to work on the two fallen warriors. Angelo however, remains close to his friend and Zuri so he can gain valuable information concerning their condition. Angelo continues to converse with the paramedics to find out whom, if not both, has been shot. Zephora refuses to sit with the rest of the ladies and remains as close by Marcus' side as possible while calling his name repeatedly in an attempt to see movement of any kind. The paramedics work feverishly on the two gentlemen and finally are prepared to get them into the ambulances and in route to the hospital. Angelo picks Zephora up from the floor, gathers the rest of the ladies and leads them to the limo to follow the ambulances to the hospital. They meet Veronica outside as she has been calming and helping to disperse the wedding guests.

"Angelo, what's their condition?" Are they going to be okay? Veronica asks.

"Roni, it looks like Marcus has taken a bullet to the upper left quadrant of his chest possibly piercing his left lung and one in the shoulder according to the paramedics. He also hit his head on the pew knocking him out with a possible concussion, which could turn out to be a good thing because it has kept him still. Ze's father possibly has some broken ribs and he knocked himself out when his head hit the floor. They will be rushing Marcus directly into surgery as soon as he gets to the hospital because he's in pretty bad shape and right now its touch and go."

"Why is this happening to us? I need to be with Marcus, he needs me with him. Can we get there any faster, please," Zephora begs.

The limo is filled with crying hysterical women, and Angelo and Veronica are doing their best to comfort the weeping ladies. Zephora's mind is racing and her heart is pounding. She is dealing with so much at one time. Her one true love is fighting for his life, and little does she know, it is the third time in the last two months; and the father she thought was dead is not and not only just risked his life for her but also

253

killed the man who was trying to ruin her present and future life. She gathers herself and takes the time to say a silent prayer: *dear Father God, thank you for bringing Marcus back home to me. Watch over him now Father God, save him now, and bring him through this challenge a new man on the other side. Help me Father God to keep my head through all of this, help me to build a relationship with my father. Grant my mother peace, and comfort her during this time too. We could all use a break Father; we have been through so much; it's in Jesus Christ Holy name I pray.*

There is no time at the hospital to stop and see Marcus as he is being rushed into surgery. Zuri has regained consciousness and his injuries are being treated by an E.R. doctor when Saphera walks in the room.

"Zuri, where have you been, how are you alive? That was you in my room when I was in the hospital. My God, it is so good to see you, I have so many questions for you but they can wait because your daughter, our daughter needs you right now. Thank you for saving her life and I just know you had something to do with Marcus making it back here from Africa. Where have you been man? I have missed you."

Saphera waits until the doctor has finished wrapping Zuri's broken ribs and butterflying and bandaging the contusion on his head before she makes a move towards Zuri. First she slaps him and then she grabs him and gently embraces him, not to hold him too tightly and squeeze his damaged ribs, while carefully and passionately resting her lips on his like it was the very first time they kissed. Zuri matches her passion with some passion of his own and looks into her eyes and whispers "I have never stopped loving you or our daughter in all these years we have been apart. I am so sorry I had to deceive you and leave you to raise our daughter on your own. You have done an incredible job and I thank you so much. I was just about to believe I would never see the two of you again. I have truly missed you and I love you so much. Now please take me to see our beautiful daughter."

Zuri and Saphera stand there in the E.R. embracing for a little while longer. Saphera releases from their embrace and slaps Zuri again. "And that's for making me think I was going crazy." She then clinches him again in an enduring embrace trying to make it last as long as possible as to make up for the last twenty plus years, while staring into one another's eyes wishing this moment didn't have to end. But, they must go and take care of their daughter who is patiently waiting for answers. They walk out of the E.R. cautiously with Saphera draped on Zuri's arm looking like a couple in love. As they walk into the sitting area, Zephora is standing, still in her wedding gown with patterns of blood, Marcus' blood and even some of Zuri's blood, splotched across the front, and turns to see her mother and father together for the first time ever. Zuri, with so much compassion in his eyes, softly speaks her name, "Zephora, my baby," and reaches out to hug her and she returns his welcoming gestures with her own and responds with a reciprocating "Father." The three of them sit down with Zephora sandwiched between them. Zuri inquires if she has heard anything about Marcus' condition and Zephora drops her head and says "No." Zuri is living the moment he has dreamt about so many times in his mind and it was going just like he imagined it would with the exception of Marcus being in the hospital fighting for his life.

Across the room Angelo and Veronica are taking the time to catch up while Charlie curls up and falls asleep on a sitting area two seat chair exhausted from all the drama.

"Well Roni, Angelo starts, we have got to stop meeting like this. Our first date was in this very room; I guess it is only fitting that we have another date here as well. Maybe we can make it a bi-monthly thing. So, can I get you anything?"

"You are so silly. No thank you, I'm okay right now. And you are absolutely right Angelo; this is the most opportune place for another date; however, let's make sure the next one does not include someone we know being injured and treated here. So tell me you handsome man, how have you been the last couple of days since I've seen you?"

"As good as a man in love can be while trying to run Marcus' business while he was off defending the honor of his fare lady. I have been importing and exporting my butt off and enjoying every moment of it. I did find time to think about you even though I was unable to call. How did you fill your time over the last couple of days?"

"Well my handsome man, it sounds like you had an interesting time. I, on the other hand, spent the last two days consoling and preparing my best friend to marry that African goon Kwazan. Sometimes she wasn't crying and we actually were able to share a laugh or two. However, I must say, I too found time to daydream a little about you as well."

"I really haven't met anyone quite like you before Veronica, and if I have my way, I do not plan on letting you get away."

"I must say Angelo; I am taken by you as well and surely would love to continue forward in our relationship as well. However, we do not have to continue doing it here at this hospital."

The two of them enjoy a laugh and continue talking. Marcus has been in surgery for several hours and still there is no word from the doctors about his condition. Zuri has been keeping everyone's mind off of the current situation by telling the story of Marcus' escapades in Africa, and he and Charlie's travels in the Bahamas. Finally the doctor comes out to tell the family of Marcus' condition. He starts with a complimentary greeting.

"I'm glad everyone has decided to stay and I'm sorry it has taken so long for me to fill you in. Marcus took a bullet to the chest as you know and one to his left shoulder. It was a delicate situation but we were able to remove the bullets, stop the internal bleeding, and repair the damage to his lung. He will need months of recovery but the prognosis is good and we expect he will make a full recovery. He is in the recovery room now and resting. Once in his room, I can allow one person at a time to go and see him for a short visit. He needs his rest.

Zephora walks in Marcus' room and bravely holds back the tears as she moves closer to his bed. She pulls over a chair, sits and takes hold of his hand and moves in to gently press her lips gently against his forehead. "Rest easy my king; I will be right here when you wake up. I am so very proud of you; you are my hero and I love you." Marcus has tubes coming from his nose, mouth and chest, machines and monitors connected to him and a bandage on his head. As he lies there half-conscious Marcus could hear the words of his love, his queen, his life, and though he was unable to open his eyes, he gathered the strength to move his index finger across the top of her hand, bringing a smile to Zephora's face. She rests her head on his stomach as her tears roll down her face and onto the side of the bed; and the two of them slept there for the rest of the night. Charlie poked her head in the door to see Zephora there with her head on Marcus and decides she will just see him in the morning.

Angelo also looks in on Marcus and notices Zephora sleeping with her head resting on Marcus' stomach and returns to the sitting area to let the others know what he has seen. Zuri and Saphera elect to go back to Saphera's home to catch up on lost time. Veronica and Charlie stop by Zephora's to pick her up a change of clothes and then go to Veronica's place for food and sleep until the morning. Angelo takes some time to go by

Marcus' house to gather clothes for Marcus and a possession of his that Marcus has been storing there for safe keeping. He then goes to his home, showers, changes and returns to the hospital, as his place is by his friend's side.

It's 1:00 a.m. and Angelo arrives back at the hospital, and he finds Zephora in the same position as when he left. Angelo grabs a chair, places it in a corner of the room and there he sleeps watching over both Marcus and the love of Marcus' life like a true warrior and brother.

It's 4:00 a.m.; Angelo and Zephora are awakened by the blaring of the alarms of Marcus' monitors and Marcus gasping for air. Zephora runs into the hall, "NURSE, NURSE, WE NEED SOME HELP IN HERE." The nurse quickly arrives and presses the call button, "CODE BLUE, CODE BLUE." Angelo grabs Zephora and pulls her back out of the way so the medical staff can work on Marcus. Zephora is crying and presses her face affectionately into Angelo's chest. Angelo holds her tightly and assures her, "He'll be okay; you know he's a fighter. Don't worry sista, don't worry."

Marcus' breathing becomes more and more erratic and then…then he flat lines.

"NO MARCUS!! OH MY GOD, THIS CAN'T BE HAPPENING! GOD NO, PLEASE DON'T LET THIS HAPPEN!" screams Zephora.

"NURSE, GET A CRASH CART IN HERE STAT AND GET THEM OUTTA HERE, NOW!!"

Angelo and Zephora are escorted to the waiting area. Zephora can't stop crying and Angelo is pacing back and forth with his hands locked in behind his head and taking deep breaths.

"Okay, okay listen Ze, let's do what Marcus would do, let's pray." He walks over to Zephora, grabs her hand, pulls her up, grabs her other hand and they stand face to face and bow their heads.

"Our Father, who is in heaven, Holy is Your name, thy Kingdom come, thy will be done, on earth as it is in heaven. Give us this day our daily bread and forgive us our trespasses as we forgive those who trespass against us. Lead us not into temptation but deliver us from evil, for Yours is the kingdom, the power, the glory forever and ever, Amen, and Amen again. Father God we come to you in this hour of need, asking that you watch over Brother Marcus and bring him back to us. We pray that you heal him tonight Father, restart his heart, refresh

him, and grant him another opportunity to live. He does so much good with his life Lord, please save him so he and I can do more of the same. Comfort Zephora, heal her father and bless the families of any and all of our enemies. It is in Jesus Christ's Holy name we pray, Amen."

"Amen."

Just as they finish praying the doctor comes into the waiting area and gives his report. His face is emotionless and he holds his head slightly to the right.

"He's okay, we were able to stabilize him and he is resting again. He's out of danger now; one of the tubes was blocking his airways and we had to remove it. We have taken him off of the breathing machine and he is breathing on his own now. He is one tough character, and will make a full recovery. You are welcome to go back in."

"Thank God and thank you doctor," Zephora responds with a smile finally on her face. She turns and gives Angelo a hug and they walk down the hall to Marcus' room. Zephora takes her position back at Marcus' side, and now, since his breathing tube has been removed, she lets her lips rest against his for a moment, then kisses his hand and again rests her head on his stomach; she takes a deep breath and closes her eyes.

Angelo takes his position in the corner and watches over his two friends for the remainder of the morning.

It's 10:00 a.m., and Zuri and Saphera arrive at the hospital with Saphera passionately holding onto Zuri's right arm as they enter the hospital. Right behind them are Veronica and Charlie laughing as they enter the hospital. The ladies take a seat in the waiting area and Zuri goes down the hall to Marcus' room. Once there, he finds Marcus sitting up being fed his breakfast by Zephora and Angelo is asleep in the corner. He didn't sleep after Marcus' 4:00 a.m. scare. Zephora stops feeding Marcus long enough to turn around and give her father a big hug; she then goes back to feeding her man.

"So Marcus, I see you are doing well and in good hands."

Marcus nods his head and continues eating. Angelo wakes up and sits up in his chair. "Good morning sir."

"Good morning young man, how's our patient?"

"He gave us a bit of a scare earlier, but as you can see he is doing much better now."

"Thank you for staying here with my daughter and Marcus."

"You don't have to thank me; these two are family to me."

Zephora leaves the room and takes the time to change into the clothes Veronica brought for her and freshens up while Marcus, Angelo and Zuri talk in private. She then stops by the waiting area to speak to her mother, Veronica and Charlie. Zuri slips out the back door of the hospital without the ladies knowing while Marcus and Angelo catch up. Angelo leaves the room as the doctor comes in to check Marcus out. Angelo goes to the waiting area with the ladies and asks if he can talk to Veronica alone for a moment and the two go outside to talk.

It's 11:30 a.m. and Zuri sneaks in the back door of the hospital as unnoticed as he slipped out and he arrives with someone else and they head into Marcus' room. When they open the door, Zephora, Charlie and Saphera are all standing around Marcus' bed laughing and sharing their love and joy of his recovery. Angelo saw Zuri from down the hall enter Marcus' room, and he and Veronica stroll hand in hand down to Marcus' room to join everyone else. When they open the door and go in, everyone is there, plus Pastor Chappell.

Saphera shouts, "WE'RE GONNA HAVE A WEDDING, RIGHT NOW!!"

Angelo replies, "Let's make that two weddings, Veronica said yes!"

The room is filled with claps, smiles and laughter. Angelo still has Marcus' and Zephora's rings from yesterday, and when he went to Marcus' house last night he retrieved his rings that Marcus has been holding for him. He has been preparing for this day for a long time without knowing who he was preparing for; however the rings are just Veronica's size. Charlie runs down to the gift shop and picks up two bouquets for the occasion and the nurses help Marcus into a wheel chair. Marcus, from his chair, manages to find the strength to stand face to face with his beloved Zephora; the time has finally come to make her his wife and he doesn't want to wait another minute. To his right, Angelo is standing, facing Veronica; thinking to himself "He who finds a wife finds a good thing."

Pastor Chappell is standing in front of the window facing the two couples with his Bible clasped in his hands and a smile on his face. Standing at the door to the room, as to guard it and prevent any interruption, are Zuri and Saphera, holding hands, both still wearing the rings that joined them so many years ago, smiling at one another, their love renewed. Charlie is standing next to them looking happier than she has ever looked before; her life has new purpose and her thoughts are "I'm next."

It is 12:00 p.m. and the sun is high in a cloudless sky that is bejeweled with double rainbows as if to signify an end to the storms which have been plaguing their families for centuries and the beginning of a new covenant of peace. Pastor Chappell begins the ceremony but chooses to skip ahead of his normal introduction and get right to it. "Dearly beloved, we are gathered here today to join Marcus and Zephora, and Angelo and Veronica in Holy matrimony. They understand that marriage should not be entered into lightly and is a pledge of commitment between themselves and God." He stops and chooses his next words wisely as they have ended his last two proceedings; he clears his throat and with faith and God's blessings clearly states "If there are any objections to these unions speak now or forever hold your peace.................